THE DON

THE FAMILY

KATRINA JACKSON

1 / SHAE

GETTING your heart's desire can be complicated.

Four months ago, if someone had told me that I could go back to Italy — and on someone else's dime, no less — I would have been jumping for joy. But now that my dream is about to be a reality, all I feel is an overwhelming dread washing over me in the blink of an eye. I've been drifting over the past few months shoving metric tons of uncertainties down inside myself, too nervous to feel or make decisions or live, even. But as soon as the Council of Aunties decree, in one decisive old Black womanly melodic hum, that Zoe and I will be going to Italy, all that fear begins to rise to the surface. That bright flash of excitement — that might have bordered on ecstasy, if I can be honest with myself for a moment — crashes into the barbed wire fence better known as reality. This confusing mix of feelings is only made worse by the fact that my mother, aunts, grandmother, great-aunts, and great-great-aunts seem to be so damn happy to have this matter settled. It's as if they can already see Zahra boarding a plane to return home and explain her weeks-long absence.

I guess I'm glad they're happy, because I sure as hell am not.

I feel like I'm watching the Aunties' celebration and Zoe's annoyed negotiation about plane tickets from a completely different room in Auntie Ella's apartment. Every time someone looks in my direction, I feel like they can see through me — like if they want to, they can pluck all the secrets I've been hiding straight from my brain.

And then what would I do?

I've been batting that question around in my head for so long, but I still don't have an answer. Normally, in moments like this, I'd turn to Zahra, but she's MIA. Or Zoe, but she's currently huddled in the corner with her mother and mine, trying to convince them to at least upgrade us to business class for the inconvenience. They don't seem to be buying her argument, but my sore back wishes her well. Meanwhile, I am sitting in a chair in the center of the room, trying to exert enough self-control to force my tense muscles to relax and my pounding pulse to slow.

I'm failing, but I don't think anyone's noticed that just yet. As usual, I am wrong.

My Auntie Caroline slides into Zoe's seat next to me with a warm smile on her face. She reaches for my hand and squeezes it.

I can only glance at her before I feel the all-too-familiar pressure of tears in my eyes, and I have to look away.

"I dreamed about fish again," she says softly.

I shut my eyes and pray not to let a single tear fall. Especially not in this room of women who will notice and be relentless about finding out what's upset me, no matter if they upset me in the process. Families are very complicated.

"These dreams just won't let me rest," Caroline says. "At first, I thought it would be Zahra 'cause you know? But that was before...you know. Then I thought it could be your cousin Maryse, but now did you know her roommate was actually her girlfriend?"

I laugh so hard that a tear falls from my right eye, but I brush it away and cover my mouth to muffle my gasping laughs.

Caroline gives a good-natured hum. "I'll take that as a yes, then. I bet not be the last to know."

"I don't think you are," I say, squeezing my aunt's hand but still not daring to look at her.

"It's not Zoe," she says.

"Never," I say and then hold my breath, waiting for her to ask me or accuse me or something.

She does neither, and so we sit there together while Zoe pleads our case, and the other aunties start putting together a list of various Italian delicacies they want us to bring back — smuggle, in some cases — because apparently, this is not just a mission to retrieve my wayward cousin, it's a shopping spree. I should have expected that. Normally, I would laugh at my family's ability to multitask, but this all still feels like it's happening from far away — but not so far away now that my aunt is holding my hand.

We lounge in a companionable silence for a while before Caroline finally reaches for my chin and turns my head toward her. Thankfully, I've had enough time to compose myself that I'm not so immediately on the verge of tears — although with the havoc of my hormones lately, I know that could change at any moment.

"Do you want to go back to Italy?" she asks.

Caroline is technically my great-aunt, but she's always been on her Rich Auntie Vibes — the one who showed up for family events only if they fit her schedule, who never missed the opportunity to commemorate a birthday with a cute Afrocentric card and a crisp twenty-dollar bill inside that arrived at least a week early and by airmail from a new country every year. She was the auntie who showed up at the family reunions with a store-bought cake, top-shelf liquor, and a different hand-some, obviously rich man on her arm.

Caroline was Zoe's role model and the kind of aunt who always made sure to let us know that the world was so much bigger than we imagined. I can guess that she's probably the reason Zoe and I are going back to Italy when a private detective would be a better choice. I can only suspect why she doesn't ask if the fish dreams are about me.

"If you want to stay here," she says, whispering only loud enough for me to hear her, "then you can stay. Zoe can bring Zahra back on her own."

I nod because she can. Zoe can do anything on her own.

"And if you want to stay with Steve—"

I shake my head sharply, cutting her off. "We're done." Those two words still taste sweet on my tongue.

Caroline exhales and smiles. "Good. But still, you can stay, and we can move you into Zoe's apartment. No one should have to stay with their ex after a breakup. Especially not a triflin' man who won't even take the couch so you can get a good night's sleep." She shakes her head and brushes the pad of her thumb along the edge of one of my deep-set, dark brown under-eye bags. "You can do that," Caroline says. "You *can* stay here if you want to."

"But I don't want to," I admit emotionally. That teary pressure is back again.

"Are you sure? Because you were sitting here looking like you was full up of dread."

I nod because even the thought of admitting that's exactly how I feel is too much for me to handle right now.

Caroline squints her eyes and tilts her head to the right as she considers the conundrum of my emotions — my life. For a few tense moments, I seriously consider telling her everything that's been going on. With her age and wisdom, surely she'll be able to figure out how to fix the mess I've made of my life and tell me what to do next. It's been months, and I sure don't know what to do. But I can't do that, especially not in this room with basically all of the women who raised me. I'm overwhelmed enough.

"It's complicated," I tell her, slouching in my chair.

"Sit up straight," she says automatically, and I do. "Life is complicated. But hey," she says, throwing her hand up in the air. "Your business is your business, and no one here gets to tell you what to do."

"Do they know that?" I ask, mouth wide in shock at these words.

"Well," she shrugs, smiling fondly, "in theory. Look, whatever's complicating your life more than usual right now, here's what I think."

Caroline excels at giving advice. All my life, I've watched her swan into the family reunion/wedding/funeral, give everyone younger than her — including very grown women — the benefit of her years and years of life and experience, and then hop on another plane out of town long before it was time to wash a single dish. She has always had a particular knack for arriving respectfully late and leaving fashionably early, the weight of her words and scent of her perfume lingering, while an empty bottle of good liquor and untouched cake remind everyone not just of her presence but her priorities. So I don't pretend that I am above whatever advice Caroline can give. I turn my entire body toward her and watch her face eagerly, letting her know that I'm listening hard.

"Complications aren't always a bad thing. Sometimes you gotta step out on the ledge, not to jump, just to get a new perspective. And that new perspective might uncomplicate everything." She squeezes my hand and kisses me on the cheek. "Bring me back a refrigerator magnet."

"What?" I ask, laughing at the sudden change in subject.

"A magnet. I went to Rome two years ago and meant to get one but forgot. I've been mad about it ever since. Every damn time I look at my collection, I swear I see that magnet of the Colosseum I meant to get but didn't." She shakes her head and stands from her chair. "Only regret of my life, I swear."

"Only regret?" I mumble to myself as I watch her walk away. "I can't even imagine."

Surprisingly though, once Caroline is gone, I realize that I feel better, freer, somehow.

And then I think of Salvatore.

I've dreamed about him for so long that even just thinking his name brings a picture of him to my mind.— the sun hitting the dark gray strands of his hair, glinting off his glasses while he smiles at me. But for the first time, I try to imagine him here in front of the Council of Aunties.

Apparently, my entire family hated Steve, not just Zoe. The whole family. So, I can't help but wonder what the fuck they'll think of Salvatore. What will they say when they find out that I'm pregnant by someone who isn't the boyfriend they hate but a man who's definitely closer to my mother's age than mine? The married man. The man I met once for only a few hours before he impregnated me. The man whose last name I don't even know.

The man I can't forget.

I can't picture him here, and that makes my heart

break. And I guess that's an answer to one question, at least. Why aren't I happy knowing that I'll be in Italy this time tomorrow? Because the man I've been dreaming about is the ultimate figment of my imagination; just real enough that I can still feel his fingers digging into my waist, bending me forward while his tongue explores my pussy, but so completely unattainable that those memories hurt, because I'll never have more.

If I were smart — if I were Zoe — I wouldn't go back. If I were stronger, I would take the out that Aunt Caroline gave me and let Zoe go on her own while I move into her spare room and find an OBGYN and therapist. But I'm not.

I know that as surely as I know that this avocado-sized collection of cells in my stomach is Salvatore's and mine. I know that I'm going to get on that plane and go back to Naples because the memory of Salvatore watching me walk away is haunting me. No, scratch that — the entire afternoon I spent with him has been haunting me, and I don't want it to stop. I see him standing in the doorway of his restaurant, watching me rush off to the train station in my mind's eye, and I think we both knew that I wanted to stay.

But did he want me to stay?

I feel pathetic worrying over this question again, but I can't help it; it's eating me up.

Some days I'm certain that he didn't. Couldn't. I was probably just the latest in a long line of tourists he brought to that back room. Those are the worst days.

But on the best days, I imagine him standing at the

door all these weeks later, looking out onto the square, seeing echoes of me walking away, stuck in the moment in the same way I'm still there.

And that's why I'm going back to Naples. On the slim chance, the faintest brush of hope, that Salvatore has been waiting for me to return as desperately as I've been waiting to get back to him.

Salvatore

You're never too old to ask for help, Sasà.

-An Old Friend

When I left the restaurant this afternoon for a visit to the barber, everything on my desk had been as it should be. A neat stack of papers I'd collected for the restaurant's accountant, a vegetable order from the head chef that I needed to call in, a message from a walking tour company interested in bringing their tours to La Casa Colonica — a request that made Alfonso and I laugh for a good long while.

I walked to the barbershop. It was a lovely day out. The sun was high in a light blue sky. The air was crisp, a welcome reprieve after a too-hot summer. The cooler weather reminds me of spring and Shae. But everything reminds me of Shae. The high sun in summer made me think of her smile. The moon seemed to be the same shade of the palest skin underneath her breasts, wet sand the same darker shade of brown at her inner thighs, soft jazz notes the same tone of her satisfied cries in my ears, and the warm water of my shower made me think of her wet release when I stroke myself to all these memories of her. I moved through the city in a haze, not quite seeing anything around me as I hallucinated Shae's echo everywhere, just around the corner and through every window.

I've enjoyed many of these slow walks around the city in recent months, even if Alfonso, always a big, hulking wall at my back, did not. These strolls never failed to make me wonder at a life I'd only imagined in the months since I'd met Shae. Before her, I was something like content with the life I'd fought and killed for. But Shae walked into my restaurant and threw contentment out of the window.

When I was younger, hungry, and dangerous, I'd thought this life was the best I could expect because it's the only life I've ever known. But if I'd ever even considered that there was someone like Shae out there, that I could taste something as sweet and pure as her, well... But that was the Catch-22 of life. If I hadn't chosen this work, I never would have gained the money and territory necessary to live this long, or owned my restaurant, or been there on that day to spend a few hours living a life I couldn't keep and didn't deserve.

I try to untangle this gnarled knot of possibility as I walk to the barber and back, hoping as I have been for months to turn a corner and find that all of the complications of my life are settled, and I can be reunited with Shae. Instead, I return to my office and immediately know that something is wrong.

The bubble of my fantasy bursts, and I'm just an old man, staring at my desk, noting the stack of ledgers for the accountant, the grocery list, the message from the walking tour company, trying to figure out what exactly is out of place. It takes long, silent moments of contemplation before I finally see the slip of paper underneath my phone. I recognize the handwriting. I understand the message. But all I can think of is Shae. In fact, if I hadn't been so preoccupied with thoughts of her, I might have seen a familiar face on the street, some sign of the messenger who put this note here. But I was distracted — I still am — and this note is a reminder of the danger that always lurks around the corner waiting for me to let my guard down.

There are many things I deserve in life, but Shae is not one of them.

THE BABY DOESN'T KNOW that we're flying back to Italy, of course, but I do, and I feel as if I need to wallow in the importance of this trip on my tiny fetus's behalf, even though this is all about Zahra and the aunts, even Zoe to some degree. Not me, though. Certainly not this baby no one but me even knows exists.

But Aunt Caroline always says it's okay to be just a little bit selfish — a tiny bit narcissistic — and that's exactly what I do while Zoe sleeps peacefully next to me. I'm a little envious at how quickly she falls asleep, almost as soon as the plane starts to taxi away from the gate. I wish I could shut my brain off enough to do the same because I'm so goddamn tired, and sadly, the hard-won business class seat is more comfortable than my old lumpy couch. I would, in fact, love to sleep the entire ten-hour flight to Rome, but I can't. I'm awake for the first four hours of the flight, worrying over what might happen if I somehow run into Salvatore. And what I'll do if I don't. I worry over which option is better. Or worse? I have no more answers today than I did the day I found out I was pregnant.

The little nugget inside me — I think that's what I'm going to call it — is too small to know or care, so it's just my imagination and nerves that make me think the tiny avocado of cells is doing flips in a dozen dizzy circles at the prospect of returning to the city where it was created.

Eventually, hours of worry and weeks of bad sleep finally collude with the loud hum of the plane's engines to lull me into a fitful slumber. But it doesn't last. One minute I'm hugging my knees into my chest, trying not to let the rollercoaster of emotions and life trigger my nausea and gag reflex; the next moment, I'm dreaming peacefully of snuggling into a bed of crisp, sun-dried white sheets with Salvatore. We're laughing, fucking — hell, sometimes just touching and staring into one another's eyes. It's the best dream I've had about him by far, and that's a very high bar.

Dream me is so happy that real-life me wants to cry. But then, the next moment, I'm blinking awake to the sound of Zoe's irritated voice.

"Shae. Shae, wake up. Girl, wake the fuck up."

I hear Zoe in the back of my brain but from far away. I resist following her directions with all I've got, trying desperately to hold onto the peace of my dreamworld, the only place where I feel actually happy these days. This behavior is very unlike me, but it's like the people-pleasing part of my personality is offline temporarily. Or maybe it's just that nothing in the real world, not Zoe's annoyance or a just okay airline meal, can beat the dream of Salvatore whispering my name and kissing up my back as he eases his dick inside me. The Salvatore of my dreams presses his hips into my ass as he takes me from behind, his perfectly elegant hands cupping my breasts, rolling my nipples between his fingers while his mouth spills the filthiest promises across my bare shoulders. I've had this dream so many times that it feels familiar, so much better than reality. It's beautiful and comforting, but it doesn't last.

Because then Zoe's hands join her annoyed voice. "Girl, wake up! You need to eat. Your mom will kill me if you faint before we even get to Italy. And I do not have time for that." She mumbles that last sentence under her breath, but I catch it as my dream begins to slip through my fingers like the finest sand.

Zoe manages to shake me gently and roughly at the same time — her specialty. She pulls me fully awake, and I am not happy about it. Well, my brain isn't, but the rest of my body is. As soon as I'm awake, my stomach grumbles in hunger, and my back muscles begin to spasm painfully. The plane's lighting is too artificially bright, and I have to shut my eyes as soon as I open them; a searing pain shoots around the perimeter of my head. I stretch in my seat and groan as all the tense muscles in my body scream from being bunched up in this seat for who knows how long. I wipe the drool from the corner of my mouth and look around, trying to moor myself in whatever part of the trip we're in. We could be landing, for all I know.

I watch as Zoe pulls the seatback tray down in front of me and places a tray atop it. "I grabbed you breakfast. Hurry up and eat it before we land."

"I'm not a child," I snap back.

"Oh, she spicy today. I approve."

"Fuck you."

"Don't get carried away," Zoe says, shooting me a warning glare as she places a cup of coffee on my tray.

I sit up straighter in the seat and roll my eyes. "Thank you," I say, opening the lukewarm foil dish in front of me. My stomach growls again. I open the plastic silverware and practically inhale the oddly mushy veggie omelet and potatoes. I'm so hungry that no one could have told me that this wasn't a meal from a Michelin star restaurant.

I shove the last potato into my mouth and turn to see Zoe watching me with a very familiar look on her face. "I was hungry," I mumble around a full mouth.

"Told you," she shrugs.

Just then, the flight attendant pushes the cart past our row and doubles back to smile down at us. We hand over the trash from our meals. "Would you like anything to drink?"

"More coffee, please," Zoe says.

"Water, please."

She pours our drinks and goes on about her way. Zoe sits back in her seat to let her food settle. I wish I was so lucky.

"I have to go to the bathroom," I say abruptly.

Zoe sighs, taking a critical second to be annoyed before she undoes her seatbelt.

"Come on, Zoe," I whine.

"I'm going."

"Faster," I say with wide eyes.

When she finally steps into the aisle, I dart past her toward the middle of the plane. There's no line, and when I look up at the icons, I can see that one of the three toilets is free. I break out in a run toward it. I have to breathe deeply through my nose and clench my jaw. If I open my mouth, I think I'll fall completely apart, and I can't do that. I've felt like this so much in the past few weeks. Maybe I've *only* felt like this. I don't know how much longer I can hold on, physically but also emotionally.

On the physical front, the answer is not much longer, actually. As soon as I close the door to the toilet, my stomach feels like a rickety boat on a turbulent sea. I press my back against the door and close my eyes and pray for my stomach to calm. I take a deep breath in through my nose. *Big mistake.* The antiseptic scent makes my stomach roil, and I gag. I just barely make it down onto my knees and lift the lid of the toilet to throw up not just the breakfast I inhaled but everything I've eaten for the past ten hours or more, which hadn't been much, thank God.

I puke until I'm just dry heaving and feel like trash in a midday sun. When I'm finally done letting go of everything I'd just eaten — but none of my worries, unfortunately — I stand, put the lid on the toilet down, flush, and then turn to the sink. While washing my hands, I make another mistake and look at my face in the odd metallic mirror. I look fucking terrible. I would recoil at my reflection, but I'm so goddamn tired that I can't even muster the energy for that. I feel sad, and I look even sadder. I'm sweating, my mouth tastes foul, and I feel completely empty. This has got to be the rock bottom moment of my life.

But still, somehow, I can hear Salvatore's voice in my head.

"Bella."

I've never felt less beautiful in my life.

Three sharp knocks on the door make me jump.

"Hey," Zoe calls. "I brought you a bottle of water."

"You...you did?"

"Yeah. You were literally green before you ran back here."

I place my palms against my stomach, pressing down, trying not just to hold myself together but to soothe this tiny thing inside of me. I imagine that the little nugget is terrified in this moment because I'm terrified. "I was?" My voice cracks. I don't even waste the energy hoping Zoe didn't hear that because Zoe hears everything.

"Yeah, girl. I don't blame you. I'm a little queasy myself. Airport eggs were not the way to go. My bad. Do you want this water or not?"

I nod before I slide the lock open. Zoe wrinkles her nose when she sees me and, I guess, smells me.

"Ick," she says, pressing the bottle of water into my hands. "I'll grab your toiletry bag."

"Thank you," I say, definitely on the verge of tears.

"No problem." She nods and covers her mouth and nose with her left hand before pulling the door closed.

I engage the lock and breathe a sigh of relief.

I still look like shit and feel like shit.

There's no 'but' at the end of that realization.

This is just who I am now, apparently.

I see Shae everywhere.

I don't even have to try. I opened my eyes this morning, and there she was on top of me, as real as anything, her hair loose around her head like a halo, a smile on her face only for me, just like I have imagined her every day since we met. Each morning, it's harder to drag myself from my bed. But no matter, the mirage of her follows me into the shower. In my mind, she's naked and shivering in the corner, watching me while I touch myself. And then she sits demurely, naked, on my bed while I dress.

One day, I think I might cease to exist outside of the fantasy where she returns — or never left. Where I have another life. With her.

As I walk to the restaurant, I think I see her hair in a crowd of lost tourists, and I turn toward the confused cluster of people without thinking. And then I feel like a foolish old man realizing those dark brown curls were just a trick of the light, just another figment of my imagination. When the tourists continue on their way — never having even noticed me — I find myself in a sudden quiet that reminds me of her delicate laughter.

I taste her climax on my tongue all day, every day.

The time since I last saw her feels like an eternity or the blink of an eye, but neither span of time manages to dampen the significance of our encounter or the way it has unwittingly changed me. That afternoon is crystal clear in my mind's eye, sharper than so many of the years before. For the past few months, I've pushed myself to the limit, wallowing in my longing in ways I never have before. And the worst part is knowing that there's no way for this feeling to end besides letting the memory of her go.

But I refuse.

Every now and again, rage momentarily obliterates the grief. I muster up the energy to be angry that I ever met her. If I didn't know Shae existed, I could rest, I reason with myself. I could restore contentment to my life.

That anger is always fleeting.

If I'd never met Shae, I would be a different man today, certainly. I would be the man I was before, comfortable in the prison I've made for myself, cold in all of the places she lit a fire in me.

I can't go back to that. I can never be that man again. Even if I wanted to.

I walk slowly toward the restaurant feeling like a

caged bird — as if I know what it feels like to fly, but there's not enough room to spread my wings. Granted, I crafted this cage, one slain enemy at a time, one takeover after another. For years, this cage was exactly what I wanted. I didn't hate knowing these bars existed because I'd begun welding them into place long before Shae was even alive.

I never imagined one afternoon could change the direction my world spun on its axis, but now I'm certain I exist only for her.

"You shouldn't be walking alone."

I sigh and tilt my head back, enjoying the feeling of the sun on my face, even though it does nothing to warm the crisp morning air. "If you're always skulking around me, am I ever really alone?" I ask Alfonso.

"Ah, you're feeling philosophical today," he says. "I should leave you alone."

"You should, but you won't."

He shrugs.

"Did you investigate Giuseppe's problem?"

He grunts. "Extortion. I handled it."

"Hmm, interesting."

"If you say so. Not my job."

"Where is he now?"

"Right now? In a ditch in a field somewhere. Possibly."

"Hmm."

"Maybe you should have sent Giulio?" He asks that question as if he doesn't trust his judgment, but I do.

"No, I sent you, and you handled it. That is all that matters at the end of the day. Or the start, as it happens."

He grunts, but he doesn't believe me, so we settle into contemplative silence. As well as I think I know Alfonso, I have no idea what he's thinking in this moment, but I don't prod at his private thoughts. For my part, when he mentions Giulio's name, he inadvertently reminds me of Zahra. Not for the first time, my pathetic brain stutters at how much she reminds me of Shae when I am weak. Unfortunately, I always feel weak.

"Is Giuseppe alright?" I ask once I can pull myself back into the moment.

"He's fine," Alfonso says, puffing out his chest.

"Then I did send the right person for the job." I let Alfonso absorb those words because he needs to hear them. "Do we know who he was?"

"Not yet, but I'll be on the lookout for a response. I wonder who will be scrambling today."

We round the corner and set across the square toward the restaurant. The new waitress, Alma, is waiting outside, smoking a cigarette and typing furiously on her mobile phone.

"How long do you think she will last?" Alfonso quips.

"Ah, about as long as the pula wants her to, I suppose."

Alfonso huffs an annoyed breath.

"Sil gentile," I tell him.

He grunts in return. I appreciate the honesty of Alfonso's responses.

"When are they going to give up on planting someone in the restaurant?"

"Most likely never. And I appreciate the variety, in any case. Especially when they send someone who knows how to actually do the job. Buongiorno," I call to Alma.

She jumps at the sound of my voice.

Alfonso snickers. "She's just a child," he mutters in gentle amusement tinged with annoyance.

"She is," I say, looking at this woman the local police have sent in to spy on me with a sympathetic eye, even though she doesn't deserve it. "They all are." I'm speaking of Shae. She must be of a similar age to Alma, maybe even younger, and I want to look out for Alma the best I can, if only to honor Shae's memory. "Watch her," I tell Alfonso.

"Certo," he replies. I see him turn to me. His smile is surprising in its easygoing innocence. Even Giulio couldn't pull that kind of boyish charm off with a gun aimed at his temple. He turns back to Alma and waves.

Sometimes, Alfonso is the right person for the job, I think to myself.

I, too, wave at Alma, who only reminds me of Shae because I see her everywhere; they are nothing alike. Still, I pray that this isn't the snitch I have to kill. I move past her to the front door and unlock it, motioning for Alma to enter first, just in case.

I usher Alfonso inside, and his smile slips. He raises an eyebrow and gestures for me to go inside ahead of him. He cannot leave my back so exposed. I've forgotten myself in this moment; this is all part of the performance.

I'm just an old man to anyone who might be looking. And there are so many people looking.

The carabinieri, Interpol, and any number of my enemies; I have so many.

I walk through the restaurant, the smell of fresh pasta and basil in the air. I make my way to my office, my eyes going to the desk where I found the note, even though I burned it hours ago. I still need to figure out a response, but only at the right time. I'm not sure when that will be just yet, but soon. Soon.

I can feel something coming, and I'm too tired to pray that I survive it. So, I pray that Shae remembers me as a better man than I've ever been.

And then I fall into the familiarity of my routine, the cover story I've been crafting for years at a time. I take off my light jacket and hang it on the hook on the back of the door. I replace it with the same dark blue apron I always wear, even though I've never cooked a single meal in this restaurant. And before I go out into the dining room to take my regular seat at the same table where I was sitting when she walked through the front door, I close my eyes and press my right palm over my chest.

And then I think of Shae for a brief moment of calm before whatever this day will bring.

Shae

It's probably the hormones, but I swear to God the closer I get to Naples, the more real Salvatore's presence feels, which is terrifying because he has been very real to me since I left Italy all those months ago.

I mean, it's obviously the hormones and probably jet lag, but seriously, from the moment I step off the train in Napoli Centrale, I feel the memory of that afternoon I spent with him; the small smiles, his soft touches, his fingers digging into my hips, his dick pulsing inside of me before he came. I could barely handle it when there were thousands of miles between us, but now that I'm back in Naples, my pulse is racing, my skin is slick with a sheen of sweat, and my pussy — Jesus, my poor pussy — is wet as fuck.

How am I supposed to live like this?

Actually, never mind, the terrifying expectation that I could turn a corner and see Salvatore is so much better than the way I've felt since the last time I was here. The moment I left him, I felt the weight of that goodbye like a pit in my stomach, and it has only grown since. It's surprising that there's room enough for a fetus in there as well, but the nugget is still small, I guess. I was so unhappy to return home that I blamed my mood on the worst and longest case of jet lag known to humanity, and I blamed the nausea on my anxiety. But I guess both of those symptoms were actually pregnancy. Wild.

And now that I'm back, tentative happiness wars with the fear that has become my best friend.

When I used to dream about returning here inexplicably, Salvatore met me at the train station with a bouquet of flowers. Or a pizza. Sometimes wine. But now that I know I'm pregnant, it's usually pizza. I didn't eat nearly enough pizza on my last trip. But most times, I simply fall asleep and find myself in that dark room, the metal table cool against my overheated skin, his fingers leaving small bruises at my hips, and his dick so deep that soon enough, I forget how my body ever felt without him inside me.

Waking up from that perfection is harder and harder each day.

Zoe and I stomp through Naples to the tune of her maps app. We go down streets I don't remember, passing buildings that seem like all the others — ancient and crumbling, but beautiful. I can't shake this feeling that I know exactly where KeKe's coordinates are leading us, but longing and fear have warped my sense of reality for so long that I don't trust my memories of these streets or this city, only him. Still, I feel full of pathetic hope that I'm going exactly where I need to be.

Where I want to be.

Aunt Caroline might say this is intuition. But I think I'm just dehydrated and tired.

My entire body goes numb when I see the familiar storefront of La Casa Colonica. The last time I was here, Salvatore was brushing his thumb across my cheek and looking at me like he wanted to kidnap me and run away to the mountains. I wish he had. I wish I'd told him that was what I wanted, that I would have killed to stay by his side. That I'd never felt quite as safe as I had when he was inside me. But a closed mouth don't get fed, and I've been empty and starving since I walked away from him.

But now I'm back.

"What?" I hear Zoe ask. I don't even know if she's speaking to me, and I don't care because I can't tear my eyes away from his restaurant.

He's married. My brain reminds me of that terrible fact I've been avoiding like the plague since we met.

I saw his ring when he sat down at my table. It glinted in the sun when he refilled my wine glass. It was warm against my pulse when he wrapped his fist around my neck. I'd gotten off on knowing that we'd wanted one another enough to betray our relationships together, that I wasn't in it alone. I'd imagined that he was as unhappy as I was, but I couldn't bring myself to ask, because I didn't care. And at the end of the day, I'd been oddly proud of myself for doing something risky for the first time in my life, for finally putting myself first.

I'm sure it wasn't supposed to be anything more than that. And I know I'm in the wrong for coming back like this — pathetically mooning over his memory and pregnant to boot. But ever since our chance encounter, that meeting has reverberated across my life, leveling everything I thought I knew about myself in its wake.

It's so painfully naïve to hope that he felt the same, and I'm running out of time to change my mind and leave him in peace.

I see Zoe rush ahead of me into the restaurant, but I can't move to follow her. I feel rooted to these ancient cobblestones, staring at that restaurant where my life somehow changed but didn't all those months ago. I hear Auntie Caroline's voice in my head. *"Whatever's going on, I think it's 'bout time you pray."* And so, I do, but not the prayer the aunties would probably want from me. I don't pray to God to take away this burden. I don't ask Him to save me from my own sin and foolishness. I pray to God to send Salvatore to me.

I maybe should have been a little more specific.

I USED to love the days when nothing went the way I planned; when I was young and brave — or foolish — and thought nothing could kill me but the bullet meant for me. So long as I didn't end up dead by nightfall, I counted that as a successful day at work. But prosperity has changed me. I've become more calm than dangerous, more predictable than erratic. I've let myself become complacent.

My hair is more gray than black, the crow's feet at the corner of my eyes are deep grooves now, and my eyesight has begun to give way. Even the glasses I wear as props are necessary to read the newspaper these days. Somehow, I've become the sort of old man I used to see as an obstacle in my rise to infamy and power, the kind of man I killed with relish.

Aging in my line of work is a delicate dance between amassing enough power and influence to bind my foot soldiers to me and standing in the way of some other young man's ambitions. But I like to think that I'm more dexterous than other men who've stood in my shoes, even now.

Sure, I've grown soft in some ways, but so much harder in others.

I've often ruminated on the limitations of the life I live and tried to guess when, and maybe even how, it will end. This is a comfortable train of thought now, if only because my brain can wander effortlessly and unimpeded to Shae.

I'm looking at the woman in the doorway, dismissing my immediate belief that she looks like Shae, recognizing it for the same desperation that makes me see bits of her in Zahra. The woman turns and leaves, and I'm just about to turn to catch Alfonso's eye when I hear it. At first, I think I've imagined the woman calling her name, but I can't have. When I fantasize about Shae's name, I hear it in my voice. I say it with my accent and full of my lust. I don't know Shae or her name any other way. But this woman calls Shae's name in an American accent inflected with annoyance and a sense of familiarity I cannot imagine or affect. That sound makes the blood still in my veins just before it boils over, and I'm rushing from my chair.

"Non può essere," I whisper. My knee clips the table leg, upending the cup of espresso on its plate, splashing across my newspaper and my hand. I feel the hot liquid on my skin and the sting in my knee, but I don't care. Nothing can hurt more than watching her walk away.

"Shae, what the hell?" the woman calls before the door closes behind her.

It could be another Shae. I could be mishearing her, my hearing going right along with my eyesight. There are so many things that could be happening right now, but somehow, I know that it's her, that this is *my* Shae.

I can hear Alfonso calling after me, but I don't stop. There's a moment — just before my hand touches the wood of the door, just before the sun gets into my eyes, just before I see Shae for the first time in too many months — when two things become crystal clear. First, I love her. I don't care that I met her once, months ago. It doesn't matter that we only spent a few hours together. As I step outside, I finally accept what has been painfully obvious: Shae — a woman whose surname I don't know — is the only woman I've ever loved. Second, I'll kill anyone who tries to harm a hair on her head.

And then I see her again, and all I feel is an aching relief that blossoms in my chest. When it blooms, it fills all the empty spaces inside me. There were so many empty spaces before I met her.

Her beautiful lips part. Even across the distance between us, I can hear her gasp as if there's no one else in this square but us, or even better yet, as if we're back in my office and the taste of her cunt is still fresh on my tongue, her body quivering in my arms, my name a filthy prayer on her lips. I hear Shae's gasp over the sound of tourists in the piazza, the church bells tolling, and Alfonso screaming my name.

I hear that gasp because it's not a gasp at all. It's my name on Shae's lips. "Salvatore."

I'm running now. We've been separated too long to waste another minute. Not even the sound of a gunshot can stop me. In fact, I move faster, needing to get to her and make sure that she's safe.

A former lover once told me that I didn't have a heart. To be fair, she said that just after I murdered her husband, once she realized I'd been seducing her to get to him. But rage can be clarifying, allowing you to see the world from a great height. And as it happens, many women have echoed that woman's assertion, including my wife. I used to believe them. It did make sense. But now I know that we were all wrong. When I hear the explosion of that gun tearing through this quiet afternoon, I know for a fact that I have a heart because her name is Shae.

As soon as we touch, her eyes fill with tears. She whispers my name again. And I vow to never let her go.

"Va bene, bella. Sei a casa ora," I whisper softly.

5 / SHAE

IF SOMEONE HAD ASKED me if I wanted this baby twelve hours ago, I would have descended into a fit of confusion, unprepared to examine how I felt, what I wanted, what I needed. I was too consumed by despair and confusion to examine the tangle of my feelings.

I used to dream about marrying Steve and having his babies. To be fair, in my fantasies, he was a different man; better, kinder, more considerate. But somehow, over the past few months, I've moved decidedly on from that phase in my life. I can't even recognize who that version of me was, which is well and good because who I am now is pregnant with Salvatore's baby, and all the things that shaped my life with Steve no longer apply.

I have so often wondered, how can I miss something — someone — I barely got to hold? But the moment his hands grasp mine, I know that all this confusion and indecision is my brain trying to understand what my body already knew.

Salvatore might be older, Italian, married, and decidedly not mine. We might have only had that one afternoon — just a few short hours, really — but we changed each other, even the tiniest bit, and it was real.

Funny how the sound of a gun firing into a quiet piazza can put everything into perspective.

I think I go into a fugue state after that gunshot, even though I'm too numb to know if 'fugue' is the right word, what it means, or even how to spell it. Okay, so whatever, I check the fuck out of this existence after the gunshot, and I think that's the best decision I can make for myself and the nugget.

For the next I don't even know how long, Salvatore is my only constant. I sink into the feeling of his hands in mine, his sure grip holding me upright and together. I'm grateful to give that responsibility to him for a little while, or maybe forever. I don't know; I'm feeling kinda loopy.

When he leaves me, I blink back into consciousness, and I do not enjoy that. Zoe and Zahra are arguing, so at least that feels familiar. There are two men watching them warily. Someone is wheezing wetly on the table, and I do not want to focus on that at all, so I close my eyes and wait. And when I open them, Salvatore is back. I have never sighed so loud in my life.

I'm relieved for a few seconds before I recognize this room and go hot all over.

He breezes back into the room, bringing the scent of

olive oil and thyme. The mental space between the day we met and the present is so fragile that those smells and his face send me hurtling back. If I were a little more dramatic — like Zahra, no shade — I might try and convince myself that this is all a dream, but I don't. I can't. There's no time to even entertain the delusion. As soon as he returns, Salvatore pulls me into his lean, strong body and whispers more Italian to me. I don't understand what he's saying in the slightest, but my body is more than a little intrigued.

And I'm lost there for the few seconds of that hug, reacquainting myself with the spicy scent of his cologne, remembering the taste of him on my tongue, the sound of his voice growling the filthiest things to me while he fucked me so hard my throat went sore from screaming.

And I sink into oblivion again.

Vaguely, I realize we're rushing through the city — cars honking, people calling to one another across the street or out of windows, our shoes slapping against stone. I understand there's danger following us, but the only part that matters most to me is Salvatore's palm against mine.

Ignorance really is bliss.

When I step back into reality again, we're all sitting around a table in an apartment that looks very lived-in, but certainly not by any of the men sitting with us, not with all the doilies covering every surface. The timbre of Salvatore's voice is soothing, even though whatever he's saying would probably distress the hell out of me, and that's why I'm not listening. Instead, I inspect our surroundings. More doilies. Stacks of old magazines on the coffee table. Bookshelves full of dolls. Yeah, this is someone's grandmother's house. Sweet.

Zoe and Zahra are fighting again. And Salvatore is gone again. But then his hand is on my stomach, and the baby flips. Or I'm hungry, more likely, but it's nicer to imagine that the nugget recognizes that we're together as a family for the first time since the day we created it. Delusion is a hell of a drug.

"Are you sure about this?" Zoe asks, leaning toward me.

I blink at her in confusion. Did I say something? Whew, bitch, I need to eat, and soon.

"About going with him?" Zahra clarifies helpfully. "I love it, by the way," she says, gesturing toward my face and then my stomach. I clutch my arms around the belly – my baby, *our* baby. "I would stay if I were in your shoes, too." She cuts her eyes at her older sister. The three of us have been here so many times before — me stuck in the middle of whatever they've decided to disagree about today — that the familiarity sharpens my focus.

The men are across the room. Giulio and Alfonso have bent their heads forward, listening intently to Salvatore.

I can't take my eyes off of him as I answer my cousin. "Yes," I say, smiling despite the exhaustion. "I'm not going anywhere without him."

Zoe sighs loudly. Zahra squeals excitedly. Neither of their reactions matter, not really. All that matters is that Salvatore turns his head at the sound of my voice. We lock eyes, he smiles, his eyes crinkle at the corner, and my heart skips a sappy ass beat.

Zoe and Alfonso leave soon after that, my cousin looking pensively over her shoulder before she disappears through the door. I wave at her, smiling. She chews her bottom lip in worry. Zahra and Giulio leave much more excitedly, and my other cousin winks at me before she disappears. I roll my eyes.

Salvatore dips into the hallway, leaving the door open. I hear him speak to...I don't know, a bodyguard? I, of course, don't understand what he's saying, but I sink into the beauty and depth of his voice with a calm smile.

When he comes back into the room, he closes the door behind him, locks it, and then takes a deep breath before turning to me.

There are so many things we need to say. So much we need to discuss. I take a deep breath. Steel myself for whatever's coming. I'm still not ready.

"Take off your clothes, bella," he says in a rough voice.

SOME LESSONS we learn early and often; repetition is necessary. The lesson for me has always been the importance of honesty. As far as I'm concerned, it is dangerous to imagine myself as a better man than I am. I had so many chances to do better — be better. My past is littered with the debris of all those chances I never took — never even considered — because I am exactly the man I wanted to be. I started life as a blunt instrument and then honed myself into a lethal weapon to get my throne before becoming a razor-sharp blade to keep it.

Then I met Shae and discovered all the joys I've denied myself. I wove whole fantasies around her, about the limitless possibility she represented. I let myself imagine who I would be today if I had asked her to stay or, better yet, if I had followed her. I imagined a world for myself where all the sins I've committed could be forgiven or didn't exist. While we were apart, I crafted a version of myself in my fantasies about Shae; one where I was a better, gentler man. Someone who could be patient with her desire, who didn't need her so desperately that the first taste of her skin on my lips sends me into a frenzy.

But once we're alone, I have to learn that old lesson again. The danger in deluding myself is real because the danger is always me.

"Take your clothes off, bella," I tell her again. "I want you naked." I manage to gentle my voice at least, but I think we both remember that it's my hands — my body — that will be rough when the time comes.

The apartment is so quiet that I can hear her breath hitch, but it's the soft shiver traveling up and down her body that I enjoy the most. I don't want to scare her, so I keep my distance, even though I'm desperate to feel the goosebumps I can see erupting all over her skin; skin I've been dreaming of touching again since the moment she left.

"You can say no, Shae," I lean forward and whisper to her.

The shivering stops, and I hold my breath. She holds hers as well for a few long counts before releasing a loud shuddering whoosh of air.

I swallow a groan as she lifts her t-shirt slowly up her torso. Her movements are jerky at first, slow, teasing even. Her smooth skin looks even softer than I remember, and I ball my hands into fists to keep from touching her. The distance between us is not insignificant, but it's nothing. It's no longer an ocean, which means anything is possible.

She bares her small stomach to me, holding her shirt

under her breasts for a few seconds before pulling it over her head.

My mouth is dry, and I lick my lips, but there isn't enough water in the world to quench this thirst. "Your pants next," I demand.

A delicious shudder moves through her as she complies, pulling a sharp inhale through her pursed lips. I feel that sound traveling across the patch of skin from my belly button into my groin and down the length of my shaft. I'm already hard for her. I'm already drooling from the tip of my cock.

"Do you need to eat?" I ask, my jaw so tight it'll start to ache soon enough.

"I missed you," she says, reaching behind her back to unclasp her bra.

"Are you tired?"

She shakes her head quickly, and the fabric hiding her breasts from my gaze loosens.

"Are you sore from traveling?" I rasp.

Her delicate fingers pull her bra straps over her shoulders. They fall to the crooks of her elbows. She stops. Waits.

Waits for me to lift my eyes from the soft flesh of her cleavage.

I move my gaze over her chest. I see her throat move as she swallows. Her pink tongue wets her lips. Her wide nostrils flare. And her eyes widen as she steels herself to face me.

I cannot help but smile at this display, enjoying every

word, every breath, every new inch of naked skin. "Bella. Are you sore?"

"No," she whispers, her eyes meeting mine. She releases her bra and bares herself to me. "Not yet."

There's a challenge in her eyes. I'm used to women looking at me in this way — I'm certain Flavia never looked at me otherwise — but I never let it get to me because I never cared. But this is Shae, and seeing this look on her face feels like throwing gasoline on the fire she lit inside me months ago. She's shivering, and her breaths have become reedy pants. But when her back straightens, and her chin moves ever so slightly toward the ceiling, I can see that at least some of the challenge in her eyes is for herself.

She wants me to take control, and I will, very soon, but I can wait just a little bit longer. I can give her the space to rise to the occasion for herself, knowing that I will follow her anywhere.

I feel as if the weeks we've been apart have wound me up, stretching my skin taut over my body, preparing me for something I wanted but couldn't hope for, but now it's here.

"You shouldn't have let me leave," she says in a shaky voice.

"I didn't want to."

She gasps softly again and moves her fingers to the top of her jeans, tracing the outline of her lower belly. "Show me." Her voice is the most fragile, unyielding command.

I rip my hands from my pockets and take two quick

steps forward. Shae jumps at my sudden movement, but she doesn't flee. She should, but the moment for that has passed as far as I'm concerned. I wonder, though, if Shae even considered leaving because she stands in the middle of the room, shaking, waiting for me to descend upon her. She gasps when I grab her roughly and pull her to me, both of our mouths falling open on a shared, desperate, relieved moan.

I take full advantage of her parted lips with my hungry tongue and taste her for the first time in too long. I dig my fingers into her hair, tip her head back, and suck her tongue into my mouth.

I don't have to wonder if she wants this when she presses her shivering body against mine, wraps her arms around me, and pulls me into her as tight as she can, as close as we can get. For now.

And that's the thing about the lies we tell ourselves. I've spent weeks pining for Shae, only coping with her absence because I knew that were she here, she would be in danger. She returns — pregnant, no less — and someone tries to kill me again, but do I send her away? No. I hardly even entertain the idea. I wanted to be someone who would choose her safety over my desire, but all it takes is a few moments alone with her to shatter that pretense. I am exactly who I have always been. Greedy. Selfish. Demanding. But now I am also hers.

I find myself without any of my masks in this kiss. I taste her with everything I have, everything I am, all the roughness of my life before, and all the softness that I have stored up just for her. And Shae meets me as my equal. Her nails scrape over my shirt before yanking the cloth from my pants to scratch at my bare back as if only nothing between us will give her relief.

And I agree.

When I know we are on the same page, I don't bother to hold back, however little I have been.

I keep kissing her and walk her into the sitting room. I break our kiss for only a few seconds so I can turn her around in my arms. I pull her back against me, and the air rushes from her lungs.

"God, yes," she groans. Shae grinds her ass against my cock, cranes her neck to kiss me over her shoulder. She lifts her hands and grabs the back of my head, pulling my mouth back down to her waiting lips.

I remember this position; the feel of her soft stomach, fragile skin under her breasts, delicate nipples, the way she squirms and cries out when I pinch them.

"Please," Shae whines, pressing harder against me.

"What do you want, bella? What do you need?" I pull back to watch her eyelashes flutter and her tongue coast over her lips as I gently roll her nipples between my fingers.

"I want to remember," she moans softly, shuddering in my arms.

I know exactly what she means, and I feel the same way.

I want to remember what it was like when we met. I need to relive that moment. I need to know that this is all real.

I place a gentle kiss on the bridge of her nose. "Si, bella. Certo."

"Please," she whines again, covering my hands with her own, begging me to massage her breasts or pinch her nipples again, anything; everything.

I kiss her forehead. "Move your hands." My words are soft, but we both know this isn't a suggestion. And by the violent shudder that cruises through her body and the moaning gasp that escapes her lips, now I know she likes it when I tell her what to do. She is perfect and maybe dangerous in her own right.

She lets me go with shaking hands. Her arms rise overhead again, and her fingers lace through my hair.

I kiss a path along the side of her face and trace my fingers around her areolae, sometimes across her hardening nipples, just enough to make her squirm, begging me with her body as she did all those months ago. I suck her earlobe into my mouth and pinch her nipples at the same time.

"I missed you. Fuck, fuck, fuck," she cries out while squirming against me. Her hands tighten around the back of my head as if she's worried I might walk away from her this time.

Never. I'm not nearly as strong as she was.

I massage her breasts in gentle presses and sometimes sharp twists of her nipples. She begins to shake in my arms, and I smile against her cheek. I close my eyes and enjoy everything about this moment; the heat of her feverish skin, the bite of her nails against my scalp, my own heart pounding. We've both been waiting so long, and I don't want it to be over too soon.

"I've sent a man to collect your suitcase," I tell her.

"Okay," she groans distractedly.

"There are preparations for our departure. They will take an hour. No more than two."

"Okay. A couple of hours is a lot of time." She's panting as if every word is a chore. Her hips are moving in an insistent circle to keep constant pressure on my cock, teasing me as surely as I'm teasing her. But her words let me know that she's very in control.

I open my eyes to find her looking at me with fire in her gaze and soft, parted lips. There's an innocent strength in her expression, and I think *this* is what I saw the first time we met. This is what I haven't been able to forget while we've been apart. This is why I'll never be able to let her go again. I did it once. That was enough.

I grind my length against her ass "Two hours isn't enough," I say, each word a kiss over her fluttering eyelids.

"It's a start," she moans, tilting her head back, pushing her breasts against my palms, stretching her delicate neck, so she can press a kiss against the corner of my mouth. "It's enough time to make me feel you."

"Si," I groan. "I'll be gentle."

"No, thank you."

I smile against her cheek, happy to realize that I've been torturing myself for nothing. I never had to lie to myself, and if I can help it, I promise not to lie to her. But that is a concern for another day.

Right now, I take her mouth, communicating the best

I can without words that I'll make the most of these two hours and every hour we have left.

I bend her forward. Her hands sink into the sofa cushions. Her back is flat, bare, and I can't stop myself from running a palm up her spine and gripping the back of her neck, just to feel her shiver at my touch.

"Please," she moans.

I'm tense, shaking with my own need. I move both hands to her soft waist, holding her tight before caressing her ass briefly and then reaching in front of her to unbutton her pants and pull them over the curve of her ass. I kneel behind her and drag her underwear down her legs. Her flesh shakes as she moves her hips left and right impatiently, begging me to strip her naked immediately, and it's still not fast enough.

I laugh and kiss her behind each knee before I kiss my way up her thighs. I bite her lightly on each cheek.

Her laugh sounds like a whispered grunt, and I imagine all the different forms the sounds of her pleasure can take, the sounds I can wring from her.

I stand over her bent back, seeing her the way I'd wanted her then — naked, vulnerable, shivering — if only we'd had the time. But we have more time now, and I take it. I watch her until she's fidgeting impatiently, rolling her hips, rubbing her thighs together, whimpering.

"Please," she whines again.

Her soft plea brings a smile to my face. I touch the skin above her waist reverently with just the tips of my fingers. I trace half the circumference of her torso lightly before slipping my hand between her legs. Her wet lips bring me literally to my knees.

I place one hand on the small of her back, anchoring her where she is while I massage her lips and clit. My cock is throbbing in my trousers. I'm so hard it hurts. I want her so badly that I press my nose and mouth between her legs, inhaling her arousal as if I need the scent of her to live.

"Fuck!" she screams. "Please!"

The need in her voice makes my blood go hot. I take a long lick of her wet pussy and know that here is where I am home.

She cries out in surprise before groaning deeply when I tease her opening with the tip of my tongue.

"Quest è il paradiso," I whisper as I lick her between each word. I notice that her pussy tastes different than I remember. I wonder if that's the pregnancy or my faulty memory. Maybe both. No matter, I'll commit this to memory and every change in her body for the rest of my life. There will be time.

"Salvatore?" she cries out.

I want to ask her if my tongue is as good as she remembers, but I'm too busy devouring her cunt. I assume, though, that she's enjoying herself by the way she's leaking into my mouth and pressing her ass onto my face, shoving my nose between her soft cheeks. I grab her hips and lick up the crease of her ass. I refuse to miss a single part of her.

If I could drown in her come, it still wouldn't be enough.

I need more.

I need to be inside her.

I stand and rip my belt open, unzip my trousers, and push them down my legs.

"Please," she whines, and I nod, pushing my underwear just far enough down my thighs to free my dick and balls.

I shove my right hand back between her legs. I smooth my left hand up her hot, sweaty back.

Every touch makes her groan. "Inside me. Fuck me. Please."

I cry out when the tip of my dick touches her wet lips. She's so slippery, it would be easy to push my fingers — so many of my fingers — deep inside her, but that's not what either of us needs. I grab the base of my shaft in a tight grip. Shae arches her back and wiggles her ass. I begin to push inside. She bucks underneath me and tries to push back faster than I want. I have to grip her with both hands at her waist as I slowly press inside of her, claiming her as I tried to do that day, even though I knew I shouldn't.

This time, no part of my brain has to worry about the danger of taking her like this. I don't have to fear what will happen if someone finds out that I've taken her when I can't — shouldn't — keep her, because it's too late. She's already mine, and she belongs with me.

I pull out of her, my dick shiny with her arousal. I use the tip to nudge her clit, trace her lips, and then leave a wet trail between her cheeks.

"Oh God," she groans as I press gently at her anus.

"Could you, bella? Have you?" My jaw is so tight it hurts.

"Never," she groans. "Please."

If I were not already compromised, I would wonder again at how someone who seems plucked from my fantasies has stumbled into my life, not once but twice. But no one, not even me, could have conjured Shae from the depths of my desires. She's everything I wanted, certainly, but I have a sneaking suspicion that she's also the woman I need, and there's nothing more dangerous in my line of business than needing someone.

But I don't care. I didn't care then, and I can't even pretend to care now.

If someone were to tell me that Shae was crafted specifically by my enemies to ruin me, I would believe them, and I would welcome ruin in her arms.

"Later," I promise us both. I drag the tip of my dick back to her pussy, pushing inside in one strong thrust. Being inside her again is like tearing myself apart, only to put myself back together again in a new configuration. We both shudder at this feeling of wholeness.

I pull out slowly, only to thrust back in hard again and again and again.

My hips slam against her ass, making all of the softest parts of her jiggle. I want to devour her, and I will. I bend forward and lick a path up her spine and then grip her at the shoulders, anchoring her writhing body so I can fuck into her with everything I have left to give.

"Yesyesyesyes," she groans into the sofa, matching the rhythm of my thrusts.

The room fills with our desperate groans and the sound of our skin slapping together. My dreams were never as perfect as this.

"So...good," she moans, fingers digging into the cushions under her head. "Missed. You."

"Say my name, bella," I grunt, letting her go with one hand to slap her hip.

"Fuck. Me. Sal...vat...ore."

She grunts my name somehow, pretty, delicate, and completely undone.

I slap her other ass cheek, this time so hard my palm stings.

Shae is beyond words now. Her cunt is holding me in a wet, quivering grip as she shivers through one long release.

I could slow down and give her some room to ride the wave of this orgasm, but I fuck her harder instead. I fuck her until she's recovered enough to fuck me back. She presses her palms to the back of the couch for leverage.

"You should have stayed away." I don't mean to say that. I'm surprised I can even speak. But her cunt rips those words from me in a rush of lust and something that must be love, even though I know less about that than how to raise a child.

Shae glares at me over her shoulder. "Shut up," she gasps, even as her eyes flutter closed and her mouth goes slack as another short but intense orgasm rages through her. "Just shut up and fuck me," she moans loudly.

"Fuck." I groan, pulling her up against me, taking her mouth as if I'll find absolution on her tongue. I don't. All I taste is the sweetness I've been dreaming about since she left and the innocence I can only corrupt.

But this is who I am and I fuck Shae hard and fast until we're covered in sweat and we know the taste of our mingled moans. I make sure there is no confusion about where we belong.

I'm SITTING on the side of the bathtub, fiddling with the water taps, waiting for Shae in a blissful calm that is as new to me as anything else I've experienced with her. I watch the tub fill with water, still tasting Shae on my tongue, still smelling her all over my skin. I don't want to wash this off. I don't want to leave this apartment, even though I know we have to.

I turn as soon as I hear her foot hit the tile on the bathroom floor. Shae leans into the bathroom with a nervous smile on her face. She's cupping her breasts as if she's afraid for me to see her. Adorable.

"Come, bella," I laugh, opening my arms to her.

Her eyes dart to my lap. My cock is spent, but the tendrils of my desire for her can change that — maybe not quickly, but soon enough, even at my age.

She bites her bottom lip, but her smile is too big to hide as she walks into the bathroom, maybe a little less nervous with every step.

I wrap my arms around her waist and pull her close. I kiss the back of each of her hands, moving my mouth back and forth until she relaxes against me. I tilt my head back to look up at her. She's smiling shyly down at me, but only for a second. She lifts one eyebrow as her left hand moves, exposing more of herself to me. I lean forward and kiss that patch of skin. Her fingers part, and I kiss more of her; her dark brown areola, every inch of her I can touch. She cups her breast, offering her hard nipple to me, and I feast on it, lick it, open my mouth wide and run my teeth along the fat of that flesh. I tighten my grip around her as she shifts to push her other nipple greedily into my mouth.

I keep my eyes on her face, noting what she likes — lots of tongue and teeth — and what she loves — when I massage her butt while I suck on her breasts — and what drives her wild — when I shove my hand between her legs and caress her clit until she's suffocating me in her cleavage.

She collapses in my arms, and I hold her up, surprised at how easy it is to smile when she's around.

I turn the taps and let the hot water cool while, I become acquainted with a part of Shae's body I always wished I'd had the time to explore. Delectable as ever.

Shae

I know it's the orgasms talking, but this is the motherfucking life.

I haven't been back in Italy a full day, but I feel more relaxed than I have...hell, maybe ever. And that was before this man ran me a bath. Five years together, and I couldn't even get Steve to boil some water for a cup of tea, but Salvatore filled the tub and sank inside with me to wash my back.

Not even in my wildest dreams did I imagine this was how our reunion would go. I could almost forget how stressed I was, but every knot Salvatore massages from my back or shoulders reminds me of all the fear I've been carrying around with me for all this time.

"I was worried," I whisper. My voice sounds as brittle as fine china.

Salvatore's fingers are coaxing a tiny but very hard knot out of my left shoulder, but they stop at my words. "About returning? I know you didn't come here to find me."

I nod. "I thought..."

He smooths a hand over my shoulder. "It is okay if you didn't want to see me again. That would have been a wise decision."

Water sloshes over the side of the tub as I whip around to glare at him over my shoulder. "What? Why wouldn't I want to see you again?"

"Why would you?" he asks, and then his eyes soften, and his hand snakes around my body. He presses his palm flat against my stomach, and the gentlest smile battles its way onto his lips.

I quickly cover his hand with mine. "I was worried that you might have forgotten about me."

He laughs and pulls me back against him, wrapping his arms around my waist, kissing across my shoulder. "Even if that had been possible, I wouldn't have allowed it."

I smooth my wet fingers over his hairy forearms. "I also thought maybe... I thought you might have done... that with other women. Other tourists."

Salvatore's arms move under my breasts and hold me tight. His laughter mixes with soft kisses on my neck. He sucks my skin between his lips.

I moan and rub my thighs together. I'm ready for him again.

He kisses his way up my neck to my ear. "I'd never done that before you."

I turn to him. We're so close that I could count each of his eyelashes, and pathetically, I would if I had the time. "So, it was..." I swallow nervously. "Was it special for you?"

One hand flattens across my stomach again. I find that touch especially soothing, and I hope this becomes a habit.

I whimper when his other hand pulls my right leg up by the knee and places it over the side of the tub. I hold my breath and watch his hand move down my inner thigh, small streams of water leading the way between my legs.

"I have been praying for the day to come when I can touch your cunt again," he whispers directly into my ear.

I shiver and have to force my eyes to remain open, so I can see the moment he does just that. But my mouth moves before my brain can stop it. "What about your wife?"

His hand stops, and so does my heart.

His palm feels like a hot weight on the delicate skin where my thigh almost meets my pussy. "Breathe," he tells me in a voice devoid of any emotion, even anger.

I don't know what to make of any of this, but I do what he says. I only get one deep breath in before his hand moves from my leg to my neck. It's so quick that I don't even have time to cry out or shift away, not that I could because he still has his other arm around my middle.

"Shae," he rasps in my ear. His voice isn't flat now. It's deep and gravelly, and it makes my heart race.

"Y-yes?"

"Touch me."

The way he says those two words obliterates the fear I've been tending that whatever we had was a one-time thing. I thought I wouldn't be able to keep my hands off of him, but he has me beat by a mile.

A long, hard mile just like the length of his long, not-hard-yet dick pressing against the small of my back.

Salvatore lets me loose just enough so I can reach between our bodies and wrap my shaking fingers around the head of his dick.

"Fuck," I groan.

He grunts when I touch him, and I like that more than I can say, so I stroke him the best I can even with this awkward angle and the hand he still has wrapped around my neck. His hold is loose but not loose enough that I can move without his permission.

My sex clenches, and I feel myself beginning to surrender to his control.

"Everything I could tell you about my wife will sound like a cliché." He grunts. "The kinds of things an old married man says to convince the pretty young woman who deserves more to let him between her legs."

"Tell me anyway," I beg.

"I never loved her. I married her for her name and her family's power. I've never been with her."

My hand stops, and I struggle against his hold, trying to turn to see him, but he doesn't let me. He laughs, gentle and cold.

"Are you serious?"

"About which part?"

"You never had sex with your wife?"

"No."

"Why?"

"I'm ruthless enough to do what it takes to get what I want, but even I have limits."

"But you... We..."

"I wanted you from the first moment I saw you. Pure need. After you, nothing else can compare." He lifts me against his body. I know what he wants because it's what I want as well.

Together, we angle his dick toward my opening, and I sink down that delicious length.

"I kept thinking I should regret cheating on my ex with you, but I don't."

"Sending you away felt like ripping my heart from my chest over and over and over again," he groans, and we start to move against one another.

"Then it was an even exchange," I gasp.

I feel him smile against the side of my head. He uses the hand on my stomach to pull me back against him in sharp motions.

"I've never had unprotected sex with anyone before you. I didn't even think," I moan.

"Neither did I. But I don't regret it. Do you?"

I shake my head as much as I can in his hold. "I want this baby," I admit for the first time to anyone, including myself. "I want our baby. I want you."

The water sloshes violently around us. If it weren't for Salvatore's hand at my neck, I would have slammed my hands on the bottom of the tub so I could throw my ass back onto him with all my might. But he holds me against him and growls in my ear, caressing my stomach, his hand moving in small circles that edge just a little bit further down my body with each stroke.

I realize now why he's holding me this way. I realize it even before his fingers brush my clit in the softest touch, not enough to get me off, just enough to let me know that he can get me off, that I'll come when he wants me to, that my pleasure is his as much as mine.

That touch is enough to make me scream.

His hand tightens around my throat. I won't forget

this feeling tonight, tomorrow, ever. I'm so close to coming there are tears in my eyes.

"If you want to leave, I'll send you home. You and our baby will never want for anything."

I shake my head and close my eyes. "Oh, God," I moan.

"This is the only time I will say this. I don't think I will be strong enough to give you this chance again. You can go have a good life and forget about me."

"I c-c-can't," I stammer. "Please let me come."

He pinches my clit, and I cry out, but I don't come.

"Do you want to go, bella? Do you want to leave me?"

"I want to fucking come!" I scream.

I brush at his hand, and he lets my throat go easily. I twist partway in his arms and grab his face. I look him directly in the eye and pant as he uses both hands to lift me up and down his dick.

"Tell me," I beg without an ounce of shame.

He leans forward, trying to kiss me, but I back away and tighten my pussy around him.

"Tell. Me." I gasp. This time it's a command.

He wraps both arms around my waist, holding me still above him while he lifts his hips up, jackhammering into me. There's more water spilling out of the tub and onto the bathroom floor. We're making the biggest mess, and we don't care.

"I want you. I want our baby. I want you to stay."

I turn forward and reach one hand to grab the side of the tub for leverage. I shove my other hand onto the back of his head, arching my back for the best angle to slam my hips down onto him as hard as I can. "Then I'm staying," I grind out before my voice turns into a whine. "Now, please let me come."

He barely brushes my clit before I cry out.

He grabs my chin with his free hand and shifts my head, covering my mouth with his. Salvatore swallows the rest of my moans before slamming into me one last time.

His grunting release tastes better than I ever dreamed.

After an hour and a half with Shae, I feel like a brand-new man. That bath was especially rejuvenating. What I wouldn't give to be able to turn my back on the rest of the world and any consequences and build something lovely and quiet right here with her. But an hour inside her doesn't change any part of my life. In fact, every orgasm I pull from her and every innocent smile she gives me only reminds me of the danger around us, pushing me to get her as far away from this city as I can.

All too soon, there's a knock at the door.

I leave Shae to rinse off in the shower. I whistle under my breath while I dry off, smiling as I wrap a towel around my waist. Before I leave the bathroom, my eyes dart to the partition just to get a glimpse of her silhouette behind the foggy glass one more time.

But that smile falls away once I close the bathroom door behind me. I call out to see who's in the hallway, and the person on the other side knocks once, waits five seconds, and then knocks again.

"Padrino."

I recognize Francesco's voice and pull the door open. There are two suitcases at his feet.

"Quello della signora," he says, rolling a suitcase into the apartment. "And Giulio packed this one for you. He told me to bring them here instead of the airport. He thought you might need some clothes before we took off."

"Ovviamente lo ha fatto," I say with a smile that apparently unnerves Francesco.

It's not as if he's never seen me smile, but this is different. Now that Shae is here, everything is different.

"Good, thank you."

"Prego," he says quickly, sounding relieved. "We called—"

I give my head a sharp shake and motion for him to leave the apartment. I follow him into the hallway, close the door most of the way, and then nod for Francesco to continue.

"We called Tommaso," he starts, carefully, saying only as much as is necessary.

"Good."

"We're ready, whenever you are."

"Did Giulio tell you who to send with me?"

"He said you'd tell me?" Francesco cringes, turning that statement into a question, clearly hating being in the middle of Giulio and me, almost as much as I'm sure Giulio hates having to take over for me while I'm gone.

I, however, find this all very amusing. "Of course, he did. Call him and tell him that this is his responsibility."

Francesco's face begins to redden. "Padrino?"

I can hear the fear in his voice. I don't have the time or inclination to tell him that fear is only a weakness if you let it rule you, but he'll learn that soon enough, one way or another. I pat him on the shoulder. "Tell him that he can call me if he has a *problem.*" I put extra emphasis on that last word. Francesco gulps, just like I know Giulio will when he gets that message.

"We will be ready in half an hour," I tell him.

Francesco nods quickly and sighs. "Is there anything else you need?"

"Si. I need you to stop by Giuseppe's and tell him I need a special order."

"Do you want me to bring it to the airport?"

"No, this isn't for me. I need him to make a delivery." Francesco nods. "Tell him to send a basket to Puglia."

Francesco frowns. "What...do you want in it? And... where in Puglia?"

"Giuseppe will know."

Francesco's face creases once again in confusion, but soon enough, he will learn that answers come only with power. And I think he's partway to that lesson because he forces his face into a look of solemn resignation and then nods once, steely determination settling his features. "Si, padrino. Is there anything else you need?"

I smile, relieved to be letting other people hold some of my burdens, at least for the moment. "Nothing." I have Shae. What more could I possibly need?

Francesco nods again and leaves. I watch him walk down the hallway and disappear into the stairwell before I step back into the apartment and lock the door.

Shae is standing in the middle of the room. She has a towel wrapped tight around her body, but she's shivering. Once again, I wish for more time, even as I know that a day, a week, a lifetime might never be enough.

She lifts her chin in that challenge again. "Who was that?"

"One of my men. We have half an hour."

She nods, pursing her soft lips. I can see the question — probably more than one — forming in her brain. There will be time for that, but not now. Not here.

I move to her, shaking my head slowly as I wrap her in my arms. When she relaxes in my hold as if she was always meant to be there, I feel a lightness because I know she has; I have known since the moment I first held her.

I kiss her forehead and closed eyelids. "I'll tell you where we're going when it's safe," I whisper.

She nods against my chest. "As long as we'll be together."

I kiss the bridge of her nose. "I'll kill anyone who tries to come between us."

She stiffens against me at those words, but only for a moment. If I weren't so focused on her body, I might have missed it. But then she relaxes against me again and wraps her arms around my back. "Half an hour's a long time," she teases, her fingers dancing along my spine.

I laugh against her tongue.

Shae

A smooth dozen orgasms in less than two hours, jet lag, emotions running high, and pregnancy?

Yeah, so I pass out as soon as I climb into the back of Salvatore's car.

I understand that there is danger around us, but to be honest, it all feels nebulous, especially compared to the reality of my sore pussy, thighs, hell, even my biceps. All of my muscles are screaming with the reminder that Salvatore might have a head full of gray hair, but his stamina is top-notch. I'm going to stop comparing him to Steve because it's like apples and diamonds, but whew, shit, I feel good for the first time in a long ass while.

So good, I barely wake up to walk onto Salvatore's private plane. I fall right back to sleep. I stir when he clicks my seatbelt into place, I think, only to lean into his side and pass out again.

When I wake up, we're descending. The soothing dip of the plane and Salvatore's heavy hand on my knee remind me that I'm exactly where I'm supposed to be. I watch the midnight blue sky through the window and feel at peace. It's such a simple, quiet moment that it's so easy to forget that this is not the trip I'd planned. I don't know what the aunties will think about this random ass turn of events, but it isn't time to confront that yet, so I snuggle further into his side.

"Buonasera," Salvatore says, squeezing my knee. "Perfect timing."

I hum and rub my cheek against his shoulder. I'm in no rush to be fully awake.

"Where are we?"

"Palermo. Sicily."

"I know where Palermo is," I say, the roll of my eyes implied by my tone because I'm too tired to move even my eyeballs.

He laughs and pats my knee again. "My apologies for doubting you."

"Will we be safe here?"

He sighs, and then I feel his mouth on my forehead. He kisses along my hairline gently.

"Say it."

His breath is warm and gentle on my skin. "I don't want to lie to you. It would be wrong to promise you something I might be unable to deliver."

I enjoy his touch, if not his words. When I open my eyes, I tilt my head back to look at him. "Then just tell me the truth. Please."

He leans forward and kisses me. While his tongue caresses mine, I can practically hear his brain whirring as he tries to figure out how to tell me whatever he needs to say without scaring me or pushing me away. He'll just have to find out on his own that I'm not going anywhere, but I brace myself for whatever's coming nonetheless. I tighten my grip on his arm and scoot closer, tilting my head so he can stroke his tongue deeper into my mouth. I don't want any room between us, and I want him to know that.

He pulls away far too soon for my liking, but I take heart in the fact that I can feel how much he doesn't want to stop kissing me. He rests his shoulder against mine and looks me deep in the eye.

"It is very likely that we will be in *more* danger here," he says. "I wish there was another way to do this, but I have always found that confronting the threat is better than waiting for it to find me."

I nod, even though the most threatening part of my life until now has been making my half of the rent each month.

Salvatore's free hand moves under my chin and tips my head back. His thumb strokes my jaw carefully. "What I can promise you is that no matter what's coming, you and our child will be safe."

I want to ask him so many questions, but I realize it's not fair. I don't know what's coming and, to be honest, I'm not sure yet that I want to know. So, I nod at him and smile, even though it feels hollow. "Okay," I whisper. "Kiss me again."

His smile feels perfectly warm against my own.

It's WELL past midnight when Lorenzo pulls into the garage beneath the luxury condominium building I've owned for at least a decade, maybe more. I'm not even sure. I can count on one hand how many times I've been here with fingers to spare. When I bought this building, I had such grand plans for myself and my life. Sicily was supposed to be my paradise, the place where I could escape the life I was building in Naples. I used to imagine myself on the pristine beaches, dipping into the crystal blue water; a world where I didn't need a pistol perpetually strapped to my side.

I never got that life. I never gave myself the time to even sketch my dream on paper. And now, I can't fathom the ignorance of my youthful fantasy. If I try, I'm sure I can recall the events that stripped me of that naïveté. But as Lorenzo and Federico lead our Sicilian team in sweeping the building and my apartment again, Shae snores softy in my lap, and I manage to thank my younger self. It took longer than I expected, but maybe this is the life I was preparing for; a place to bring Shae and our child.

Our *child.*

I move my hand under her shirt to caress her soft stomach.

No, this could not have been the life I was preparing for; my imagination was never so powerful.

Federico knocks twice on the window and pulls the door open. "All clear," he says and then sees Shae, still asleep. "I'll get the bags."

I push her hair away from her face. I hate to wake her, so I don't. I use my thumb to trace the edge of her ear down to her jaw. She has the slightest indentation in her chin, and I touch it even more lightly than the rest of her.

She doesn't open her eyes, but I feel her stomach jump in a gasp, and I smile. "We have arrived," I tell her.

"Shh," she says, and I trace the bottom curve of her smile. The trunk slams, and she opens her eyes with a frown, turning to look up at me.

"Come, bella. It's late."

"I'm not tired," she says quickly before yawning.

I find myself smiling at Shae, Federico and Lorenzo, even the ground as we climb from the car and make our way to my penthouse apartment.

Shae holds my hand tight in both of hers. She smiles at the men Federico has placed between my car and the front door. If they make her nervous, she hides it well.

Lorenzo meets us at the door. "Clear," he says with a serious face, letting me know with a single word that he takes full responsibility for our safety. I appreciate a man who doesn't shirk responsibility, and it's always nice to know who to kill if I have to.

I squeeze Shae's hand and send her inside first.

Federico places our bags just inside the door. "Do you need anything else?" he asks.

I shake my head sharply.

"We'll have two people in the hallway. We're watching all the exits and stairwells."

"Good." It's not enough. To someone who really wants to kill me, there'll never be enough security. I know that very well, but it will do for tonight, and that's all I can ask. I close the door and lock it.

When I turn around, Shae is standing in the middle of the living room, looking at me with nothing but trust in her eyes. I want to be the kind of man who deserves her loyalty. I want to repay her every day for the happiness she makes me feel; like a weight lifting from my shoulders.

"Come, my love. You need to eat."

She grabs her stomach and smiles nervously. "I forgot I was hungry."

"I didn't. I will make you something to eat, and then we will go to bed."

Her face brightens. "Hold on. You can cook?"

It will take a while, I think, to get used to all the smiling and laughter. So much happiness when I'm with her.

Shae

It's the hormones.

It's just the hormones.

It has *got* to be the hormones.

And the smell of basil. And olive oil. And garlic.

Maybe these are aphrodisiacs for pregnant people?

"Come, bella," Salvatore purrs over his right shoulder, piercing me in his soft gray stare. "Taste this."

He turns back to the stove so he misses the way those few words make me shudder.

Salvatore's making a tomato sauce he says I'll love as if this has been just a normal night and not the first time I'm even seeing him after sunset. It's surreal, and I can't shake the fear that it's fleeting because how could anything between us under these circumstances be anything else? So, while he's been cooking, I've been sitting at the small wooden table in the kitchen, staring at his back with all my attention, committing every inch of him to memory. The way his muscles move as he chops and stirs. How sexy I apparently find it when he wipes his hands on a dishtowel and throws it over his left shoulder, all serious and focused. Aphrodisiac or not, my brain decides that the scents of garlic and basil will remind me of Salvatore for the rest of my life and probably get me wet.

I feel very tired and a little emotional, but Salvatore's been muttering softly to himself while cooking, so we've both been in our own little worlds, but together. And I really love that.

But when Salvatore invites me to taste his sauce, I stand from the table and notice things I hadn't before. Like the jazz playing from somewhere, how warm my skin is, how relaxed I feel, my tingling scalp and hard nipples. I stop with Salvatore just out of reach, my fingers twitching with the desire to touch him.

This *has* to be the hormones. Right?!

"Come, bella," he calls again.

I rub my thighs together, and the friction makes me shiver, the wet lips of my sex catching on my underwear. I could, I realize, come right now, just because he said the word. And that, I know, is not just the hormones. I'm so hungry and lightheaded that I sway just a little bit as I take those last few steps to him and mold myself against his back.

"Bella?"

I can't believe how many different ways he's found to say that word and how each variation makes me feel something warmer, deeper, and new.

"I'm okay," I say, snuggling my cheek against his strong shoulder. "I'm just tired and hungry, and I think my hormones are going wild."

"Wild?" he asks, his body swaying as he stirs the sauce on the stove.

I turn my face to smile into his back, pressing my nose into the hard space between his shoulder blades, and hook my thumbs through the belt loops on either side of his waist. "I'll tell you after you feed me."

He chuckles lightly. "I am feeding you no matter

what." He mutters something in rapid-fire Italian. "Sit. The pasta is almost done."

"I thought you wanted me to taste the sauce," I mumble into his left shoulder, in no hurry to let him go. Unfortunately, my rumbling stomach betrays me.

"Sit," Salvatore says, his voice full of both warmth and impatience. "It will be good. I promise."

I reluctantly let him go and resume my seat. I feel parched after only briefly touching him and take a long gulp of water. I put the glass on the table. Salvatore turns to eye it and me. He mutters something under his breath as he walks to the refrigerator.

"What are you saying?" I ask while he fills my cup.

"I'll tell you after you eat," he laughs.

"Liar," I mutter under my breath, but I'm smiling.

He puts the pitcher down on the table and then bends over, brushing his mouth across my forehead. "I've been called worse." He presses the now-full glass of water into my hands and returns to the stove.

I smile at his back and gulp most of the glass down in a few sips.

"So, do you cook at the restaurant too?"

He shakes his head. "No." He says that word lightly as if it's a joke, one that I clearly don't get.

"Why not?"

He throws the almost-cooked pasta into the pan and begins to toss it in the sauce. I lean to the side to see what I can, suddenly mesmerized.

"But if you know how to cook..." I ask.

He deposits the pasta into a bowl on the counter next

to him. My mouth waters, watching him grate a small mountain of parmesan onto it.

"A little more," I groan when he tries to stop.

He laughs, grating until I'm satisfied. He's a flutter of elegance after that as he sets the table in front of me — the large bowl of pasta, smaller bowls for each of us, a salad he chopped while I was sitting in this same chair doing little more than lusting after him.

"I could get used to this," I mutter under my voice as he dishes some pasta into my bowl.

"This is nothing," he says nonchalantly.

I place my hand on his forearm, and a few leaves of lettuce fall onto my salad plate. He asks me a question with just a dip of his eyebrows.

"You're underestimating yourself," I tell him. "And overestimating how terrible American men can be."

He grunts that compliment away. "Italian men can be terrible as well," he says gravely. "You must trust me on this."

I sigh, seeing how we've talked ourselves into this corner. I want to say that he's underestimating how bad my last relationship was. I want to finally tell him that meeting him forced me to face all the things I'd been avoiding for years, but I don't want to mention Steve to Salvatore and ruin the mood.

And for his part, I can see the warning he's trying to give indirectly. I know what he means, what he wants me to understand. He's been called worse than a liar. *He* can be terrible.

"Not to me, though," I say, thankful as fuck that Zoe

is not here to hear this foolishness come out of my mouth. I mean, I believe it — I don't know why, but I do. But I also know that I sound like a fool. I don't take those words back, though.

He sits heavily in his chair. His face is flushed red. I might have assumed that it was just the heat of the kitchen, except he's avoiding my eyes.

I squeeze his arm.

He grabs my hand in his and kisses my palm and the back of my wrist. "Not to you. *Never* to you," he whispers against my skin. "Now eat. Please."

I MAKE sure Shae eats as much as possible. I try not to count the number of hours since she likely last had a proper meal. That information might take years from my life, and I couldn't bear it; not now.

Besides, I have the distinct feeling that if I try and ask her how long since she last ate, she will lie. Maybe not convincingly, but she would try, and I don't want to force her to tell me what I already know. So, I keep piling pasta and salad in front of her and even feed her from my own plate until she finally pushes my fork away.

"No more. I can't," she groans. "I'll burst."

"Are you sure? Just a few bites more?"

"I'm full," she whines. "There's no more room. The baby takes up so much space."

I sit back in my chair and frown at her. She smiles wearily at me.

"Now who is the liar?"

"I'm not lying!" she cries adorably. "The baby is like this big." She holds her hands in the air, her palms far enough apart to fit a melon in the space between.

I squint at her and shake my head. I wipe my hands on the dishtowel I threw over the back of the chair on the other side of me and then reach into my back pocket. I open the pregnancy app that I downloaded while she was asleep on the plane and turn the screen to face her.

Her eyes widen in shock, and she looks from the phone to me. "Avocado. The baby is much smaller than you want me to believe. You can eat more."

"I—" she starts before shaking her head. "You."

"Si. I think our avocado needs more food."

I'm shocked into speechlessness when she bursts into tears.

I've been shot more times than I can count. I've been stabbed even more times than that, I assume; I stopped keeping count long ago. Once, maybe two decades ago, I awoke to a rope around my throat. I killed the man holding it, but I couldn't speak for days, the skin around my neck was tender for weeks, and for months after, I couldn't bear to wear anything close around my neck. It was agony.

Still, nothing shreds me quite as neatly as Shae's watery eyes and trembling lower lip. I assume this is the hormones and exhaustion, but the particulars don't matter. I pull her from her seat and cradle her in my arms. "Va bene, amore mio," I whisper, rubbing her back as she cries.

"I'm sorry," Shae sobs into my neck.

"Why?"

"I don't know why I'm crying. You're just so sweet," she wails.

I laugh into her soft hair. "No one has ever used that word to describe me, not even when I was a child."

She shakes her head and presses her body closer to me. "You've always been sweet to me," she breathes against my neck, her soft breath rustling the very bottom of my beard, threatening to make me hard in an instant.

"No, bella. I have been anything but *sweet* to you."

My voice is rough as I admit this, but I can picture her now, bent over the table in my office, her sex wet and open, waiting for me to push inside of her. I can remember the sharp gasp when I did. The taste of sweat on her skin. The feeling of her cries when I wrapped my hand around her throat to keep her firmly in place so I could fuck her until my old wound was a stinging line of fire. A sharp pain that barely registered because nothing was more important than pulling one more orgasm from her by sheer desperate will.

Right from the beginning, I have been anything but sweet, and I don't think that will change because now I'm hard, and her firm ass is sitting right on my dick.

And I think she follows the train of my thoughts when she shivers in my arms, and her soft lips move over the skin she's wet with her tears.

I still, waiting for whatever she will say to that admission, but her only response is to lick a path up the side of my neck and suck my earlobe into her mouth.

"Fuck," I hiss, wrapping my arms fully around her now.

"Salvatore," she moans.

I shake my head wearily, even as my body has begun to harden. "You need to sleep." I squeeze her side, not for any other reason than to revel in her softness.

She licks up the shell of my ear. "I know," she moans. "I want you to fuck me to sleep."

How can I say no to that? "I should clean the kitchen." A pathetic attempt.

"Tomorrow," she says, her lips and tongue moving lightly over my skin.

"Bella," I groan, my patience wearing dangerously thin. I'm tired as well.

"Don't you want that? Haven't you been dreaming about it? About cooking me dinner and then crawling into bed with me? All those things we didn't have time to do?"

"And more," I say, my voice so hoarse it scratches my throat.

She kisses me on the tops of my cheeks, cradling my head in her hands, pulling my face close before moving so we can look one another in the eyes. "Then come to bed with me. Please."

"I don't know how you do it."

Her eyebrows bunch together adorably. "Do what?"

"Be vulnerable." That was the thing that drew me to her all those months ago, her nervous smiles and bright eyes and all that damn innocence. I wanted her then with every fiber of my body, and somehow, tonight, I want her even more.

"I wish I was like this all the time. I wish it was easier to tell people what I need, but I—" She shakes her head, her eyes shifting away from mine. "It's not. I learned really quickly with Steve not to...bother."

I hate the pained frown on her face. I've never met this man, but I could kill him. I probably will if I get the chance.

"He didn't make it easy for me to be vulnerable. And since he was the only person I ever dated..." She cuts herself off again with a shrug. I doubt she even realizes that's what she's doing, but I do. Even just mentioning his name made her tense in my arms when she had just been so soft, practically melting against me.

"Shae," I whisper, squeezing her waist again.

Her eyes shift back to mine. Her smile is small and nervous again. My heart aches. "It's different with you," she says softly. "I don't know why, but it is."

She looks so fragile in that moment, her voice so brittle, her eyes watery with doubt.

I don't want her to ever doubt me. "I am also different with you," I admit. "Let's go to bed."

She takes my mouth with a hunger that matches my own. I lift her into my arms and carry her from the kitchen. I don't break our kiss. I know this floorplan by heart — it's easier to escape an attempt on your life if you don't have to turn on the lights to find a door. I never imagined using that knowledge in this way, however. Everything is better than I could have hoped with Shae.

By the time we make it into the bedroom, I can hardly keep ahold of her. She's wrapped her legs around my waist and is squirming in my arms, scraping her teeth over my lips and tongue and grinding the cleft between her legs against my stomach.

"I want you inside me," she moans into my mouth before sucking my tongue into hers, making it impossible for me to tell her that I feel like I've been waiting all my life for her, that I'm just as desperate as she is. That I don't understand it either, but I never want to let her go.

So, I tell her all of that and more with my hands. I touch her everywhere I can; her back, her hips, her ass, my fingers between her legs.

When she grinds into me with a breathy moan, I suck that exhalation from her tongue. She tastes like tomatoes and olive oil and my future.

"Please," she begs softly, shredding me to the core just as she has been since the moment we met.

As gently as either of us will allow, I pull her from me. She whines when her feet hit the floor. Her fingers twist together behind my neck, and she licks into my mouth. I kiss her back even as I move my hands to hers and gently pull them apart, holding them to my chest.

"No," she breathes when I break our kiss.

"How can I give you what you want if you never stop kissing me, bella?"

"You'll figure it out," she replies, smiling against my mouth.

I laugh dryly. Unfortunately, she is not wrong. "For

you, I would," I say, grabbing her face and tilting her head back so I can kiss her deeper.

She's bouncing from foot to foot excitedly when I pull away.

"Were you this impatient when we met?"

"Yes. You couldn't tell?"

"I thought you were nervous. I wanted to set you at ease, but I also wanted to devour you whole."

She shivers. "I remember. Get naked," she demands in a voice as unstable as the rest of her body. "I-I'm sick of waiting."

I could laugh. "Waiting for what, bella?" I ask incredulously.

"You."

How can I say no to that?

Shae

It's the hormones again. Even before I was pregnant, it was the hormones with Salvatore.

We undress quickly like giddy teenagers about to have sex for the first time. When we're finally almost naked together, I let my gaze run hungrily over his body. I reach for his face and bracket his head again. My fingers brush the sides of his glasses.

"Can I?"

He nods, his hands finding my waist.

I lift his glasses from his angular nose, carefully folding them. I have to twist away to place them on the bedside table, but his grip on me doesn't loosen. He doesn't let me get away. When I turn back, he pulls me close. I start squirming again, this time against the soft column of his dick between us. He groans helplessly, and I smile.

"Wait," I breathe.

"Oh, now you understand patience?"

I don't answer him. I'm too busy smoothing my fingers over his mostly salt salt-and-pepper beard and the flat line of his mouth.

He licks the pads of my fingers as they pass.

I move down his neck, over his Adam's apple, and then his broad chest through the dusting of graying hair. His hands twitch, and he backs away, trying to hide himself from me.

When I look up at his face, he frowns. "You're so young and beautiful. I don't deserve—"

I roll my eyes and reach down between us.

"Fuck. Shae," he gasps in shock.

Once I wrap my hand around his shaft, I realize that he's not fully hard yet, and I prefer that, to be honest. I haven't had time to focus on his arousal yet, depriving both of us. I begin to stroke the length of his shaft, squeezing him from root to tip.

His head falls back on a groan.

I lick his Adam's apple and squeeze the head of his dick. "Do you want me?"

"Need you," he corrects quickly.

"I hoped you'd say that." I twist my wrist, and he cries out.

His hands move from the small of my back, roaming all over my ass. His fingers dip between my legs again, and I let him touch me, but only for a few seconds before I wiggle my ass dislodging his fingers. I can't let him push inside me before I make him hard or I'll lose all coherent thought. Again.

He grunts and glares down at me.

I tighten my hand around his shaft. "Get on the bed."

I realize that he's dangerous, even if only in the abstract. He's certainly powerful, and I can feel all that danger in his glare. So, I also feel when he decides to give some of that power to me. Steve never did that.

He squeezes my ass cheeks one more time and nods before letting me go.

Speaking of giddy. I step aside while he crawls on the bed. "On your back," I tell him, vibrating with anticipation.

"Si, bella."

I crawl onto the bed next to him, sitting back on my heels. There is so much to see. His hardening dick lifting toward the ceiling. The salt and pepper hair on his head, face, chest, and at the base of his dick. I want to touch him everywhere. I feel spoiled for choice and desire in a way I never have before. I finally know how Salvatore has felt, I think, because I want to go slow and tease him. Unfortunately, I don't have even a fraction of his self-control.

So, I *want* to go slow, but I practically launch my mouth onto his dick.

"Merde," he screams as I inhale half his length with a happy gasp.

I grip him around the base and suck him as I lift my mouth.

"Shae. Fuck," he moans.

I'm not sure if he's asking me to stop or slow down or what, but I'm not particularly worried about that because I plan to do it all. I didn't spend hot, sweaty nights on that lumpy ass couch with my fingers buried in my pussy, straining my neck to lick my nipples, dreaming about swallowing Salvatore's dick for nothing.

I swirl my tongue around the head, dipping into the soft slit, tasting his precome with an excitement that I can only express with a happy wiggle and then a yelp when his palm smacks against my ass.

I try to tell him I like that, but I'm too busy shoving my mouth down his length again. I use my mouth and hand on him now. It takes a while to find the right rhythm, to pull my fist and lips together and apart slow enough to make him groan and then scream. But I get there.

And while I work on that pacing, his long fingers explore my opening, massage my clit, and even tease my ass. I'm panting almost as hard as he is.

But when we find our rhythm, it's even better. He curses me and the air and God, I think, and I join him when he hauls me on top of him, my pussy right over his screaming mouth.

I fall asleep knowing what Salvatore's orgasm tastes like on my tongue, feels like dripping down my chin, and how good it is to let him press my face into the covers and fuck me from behind.

He thinks I'm young and beautiful, and I think he's old and experienced.

We're a perfect match if you ask me.

I WAKE up feeling like Polly-fucking-anna. Everything is beautiful. Life is amazing. I have never been so deliciously sore in my life.

When I open my eyes, no shit, the first thing I see is a rainbow reflecting on the wall from the window next to the bed. I only saw the bedroom briefly last night, but this morning, I take in the calm gray walls, the neutral-colored oatmeal carpet and white shutters. It looks as unlike the apartment in Naples as I can imagine. That place looked like an elderly woman's home, and this place is clearly a luxury condo.

But neither of them feel like Salvatore's home.

I can't imagine him decorating any place, and so I have to wonder, unfortunately, if his wife decorated this apartment. If she bought the bed we fucked each other in last night. If she picked out these sheets I clutched while he was fucking me doggy style. If she chose the pillows I slept on. Actually, no, I don't think my head ever touched any of the pillows because I wake up with my cheek on Salvatore's slowly rising chest, my head moving as he fills his lungs and releases. I'm almost certain I dreamed about the rhythm of his heartbeat.

So, there's that, for whatever it's worth.

I feel rested, really rested, for the first time in a long time, even before I chose to sleep on that lumpy ass couch. I ache all over and reluctantly roll off Salvatore's body. I finally touch one of the pillows his wife may or may not have bought, throw my arms over my head, and stretch my limbs, yawning loudly into the quiet room.

Salvatore stirs and turns automatically toward me. He gathers me in his arms again and cuddles me into his side.

"Buongiorno," he says in a hoarse voice, his breath rustling my hair.

"Morning," I reply, sounding just as hoarse as him. Maybe even a little more so. I spent a lot of yesterday moaning and screaming, and the memories make me smile wide as hell. I press my face into the crook of his neck. Not really to hide my smile, just to feel him.

"Did you sleep well?"

"So good," I mumble.

"Are you still tired?"

I wrap my arms around his torso, my palms smoothing over his skin, thinking. "No, I think I'm okay."

His palm covers my stomach. "Still," he says, pressing his mouth against my ear through the tangle of my hair. "You should rest."

I nod and scoot forward against him, throwing a leg over his stomach. I'd do damn near anything he told me to do right now, but I'm not foolish enough to tell him that. "Are you going to rest with me?" I ask instead.

That hand on my stomach begins to move south. His chest is rising faster now. My heart is racing.

A loud knock on the front door ruins this moment and I let out a string of frustrated curses.

Salvatore laughs and brushes his mouth across my cheek before he crawls out of bed.

"Come back," I whine, turning to reach for him.

His eyes go to my bare breasts. His smile goes slack. His dick is not completely soft.

Whoever's at the door knocks again.

"I will be right back," he says. "I promise."

I watch him hungrily while he bends over his suitcase to extract a pair of sweatpants and a t-shirt. I'm a little bit angry, but it's hardly noticeable under all the lust.

"I promise," he says again, closing the bedroom door behind him as he leaves.

Not to be too pathetic, but I watch the door for at least a few minutes, hoping he'll come back, like, immediately. When it becomes clear that he isn't, I crawl out of bed and mope to the bathroom.

I look a mess. Like a fucked to within an inch of my life mess, but also a dehydrated, jetlagged, didn't put on a bonnet last night mess.

"Jesus," I mutter to myself and walk back to the bedroom. Salvatore still hasn't returned — it's been twenty seconds, but still — and I pull my suitcase onto its side.

Because the aunties were doing the most, I had to pack in a hurry, and I feel like half a year's worth of shit has happened since then, so I really don't know what's in here. I start to pull everything out. I don't know how long this trip will last, but I guess it can't hurt to hang up all these dresses I apparently threw into this suitcase for no real reason. And I just have to sigh when I realize that I've committed my mother's — and Zoe's — cardinal offense for traveling. "Where the fuck is all my underwear?" I mutter under my breath, holding up barely a week's worth of panties if I count half of the bikini I wasted time packing.

When all the clothes are piled on the floor, I take stock of my paltry ass pickings for clothes for a trip that has run off the rails in a day — assuming it was ever on the rails.

But I did pack what looks like all my skincare and a good conditioner, so there's that.

I grab my toiletries and head back to the bathroom. I leave the door open for Salvatore, just in case.

I come from a family of women who believe in caring for your body as a form of self-care. There's a lot of long soaks in the bathtub when your co-workers are getting on your nerves, washing and deep conditioning your hair when your partner is being a dick, and extensive mask usage when life is too goddamn much. The hard lesson of adulthood was that none of these rituals made me feel any less stressed or got me a better job, and they certainly didn't get me away from Steve a day sooner, but they always felt good and sometimes that was even enough.

Normally I duck and dodge the water while showering, but when I get to walk fully under the spray, it's heavenly. I'm normally a detangle-before-I-wash kind of girl, but I'll just have to make do today and be extra careful. I wet my hair and carefully use my fingers to part it down the middle. I thank my home training that I remembered shampoo and conditioner as I squirt a healthy amount of the former into my palm. I close my eyes and carefully use the pads of my fingers to work it into my hair and across my scalp, giving myself a cleansing massage.

With my eyes closed, the water beating on my breasts and stomach, and my fingers working in my hair, I think of Salvatore. It takes forever and gallons of water to wash and condition my hair and my body, but I do it all with a smile on my face. By the time I'm clean, I'm not even mad that Salvatore jumped out of bed when things were about to get interesting and hasn't joined me in the shower because I feel fucking great. I feel like brand-new.

When I pull back the shower curtain, I find Salvatore leaning against the doorjamb in an immaculately pressed pair of black slacks and a matching linen shirt. His arms are crossed in front of his chest, there's a greedy smile on his face, and a healthy bulge in his pants.

"No fucking way was I in here long enough for you to get dressed and look this good."

"You were, actually."

"But where did you get dressed? How did I miss it?"

"There's another bathroom," he says. "I would have given you a tour last night, but we were...preoccupied." He smooths a hand over his mouth, almost hiding the smile. His glasses are fogging up a little, but I can still see his eyes travel down my body, reminding me that I am very naked. And wet. And not just from the shower now.

"You could have joined me," I whisper.

The smile falls from his face. He crosses his arms over his chest. "I wish that I could have."

"You couldn't?"

He's frowning now. "No, bella." He steps into the bathroom and takes one of the towels from the rack, opening it for me. "Come."

I step carefully out of the shower and let him wrap the towel around my body.

Salvatore begins to towel me dry, making me shiver.

"Not my hair," I tell him when he turns me around.

"Si, Shae," he says in a tone of voice that makes me wet and a little scared all at the same time.

My breath is shakier than my legs.

Cool air slides up my back when he takes the towel away. I cover my breasts, even though he's seen every-thing there is to see. He tosses the towel on the floor and then, looking over my toiletries, snatches the bottle of lotion from the pile on the bathroom sink. He holds it up and looks at me to check he's chosen the right thing.

I smile and nod eagerly.

There are goosebumps all over my body, even in places where I didn't know that was possible. My clit feels like one hard, shivering goosebump that I'm desperate for him to touch. I hold my breath while he squirts some lotion into his hand. He warms the lotion by rubbing his palms together. We watch each other as he moves behind me again, brushing the ends of my hair over my shoulders with the backs of his fingers and then pressing the palms of his hands against my skin.

I jump and let out a sharp cry. My sex clenches.

"I have to leave for a little while," he says as he begins to smooth the lotion into my back.

All I can do is whimper in response.

"Where?" is the only word I can get past my lips.

He presses the last of the lotion into the small of my back before moving down to cup and caress each ass cheek in turn. I moan in a breathy, horny, needy exhalation.

And then his hands disappear.

I turn and watch him squeeze more lotion into his palm. He warms it again before looking me deep in my eyes. "I cannot tell you that, bella. I'm sorry."

I shake my head quickly, water droplets flying everywhere, on me, on Salvatore. He smiles as if it doesn't matter because to him, I don't think it does. "It's okay."

"No. It's not," he says firmly. "If I could stay or take you with me, I would."

"But you can't." It's not a question. I believe him. I *trust* him.

He shakes his head as he walks the few steps back to me.

"Will you be gone long?" I ask just in time for him to kneel down beside me and begin to lotion my right leg. I gasp and close my eyes as his hands massage my ankles, calves, the back of my knees, my thighs, my inner thighs.

"Fuck," I grunt as he lets me go again.

He has a mischievous smile on his face when I look down at him. He's getting more lotion.

I shift my body so he can reach my other leg, and I can flash him my pussy.

"Not long," he says, starting with my ankle again. "I'll be back as quickly as I can."

I nod. His fingers are tickling the back of my knee and up my thigh.

"What will you do while I'm gone?"

"Please," I whisper, my gaze locked on his thumbs, pressing into a sore muscle.

"Bella."

"What?"

He laughs. His hands keep moving up my body. "I asked what you will do while we are apart?"

"Who cares?" I gasp when his fingers brush the lips of my pussy. My entire body shudders. My voice shudders.

Salvatore begins to stand and presses a kiss on my hip before going back for more lotion.

"Come on," I cry softly, turning and grabbing him around the waist.

He rubs his palms together but turns to me, still smiling.

I whimper, and he leans to the side so we can kiss briefly, just his lips against mine before my tongue snakes out to taste him. He opens his mouth to kiss me deeper and I think I have him – that I've won – but then he backs away, leaving me panting with need.

"Cruel."

"You are not the first person to call me that either," he says, massaging the lotion into my stomach. We're eye to eye now, almost pressed front to front. His hands are moving toward my breasts. My nipples are so hard they hurt. "But usually, when someone calls me cruel, the circumstances are very different."

"They better be," I say in an unexpectedly feral voice.

Salvatore's face lights up. "What will you do while I'm away, bella?"

His fingers are caressing the delicate skin under my breasts, but they've stopped moving up. He's waiting for an answer, teasing it out of me.

"I need to finish doing my hair."

"How long will it take?"

That question wipes the smile from my face, and I stiffen in his arms. Salvatore's eyes squint as he focuses on the change in my mood.

When Steve and I first moved in together, he used to frown at me every wash day, huffing out annoyed breaths when I queued up the collection of podcasts I'd saved for my one day off when I could detangle, wash, deep condition, and twist my hair. And because it was my one day off, I'd take a bit of extra time to exfoliate my entire body and hang out in a sheet mask while I painted my nails and toes. Steve complained that I ignored him the entire day and then every week after that. He pouted and threw silent tantrum after silent tantrum until, eventually, I gave up. I lived in braids, and when I needed to take them down and wash my hair, I decamped to Zoe's or Zahra's apartments for a good wash and relaxation day. I called it a Girls' Day, but in hindsight, it was really just my pathetic attempts to keep Steve happy at my own expense.

For months, I'd been tossing and turning on that terrible couch, wondering why I hadn't broken up with him earlier. The autopsy of my relationship was a terrible thing to confront. So many red flags I didn't just see but planted in the ground myself and still ignored.

"Bella?" Salvatore says gently, his voice pulling me back into the moment, his fingers caressing my ribs.

"I won't take long," I say warily.

Salvatore's jaw tics in annoyance. The tips of his fingers press against my chest.

My breath hitches, and I squeak as his palms finally cover my breasts. All the tension of remembering Steve flows out of me.

Salvatore begins to roll and pinch my nipples between his fingers.

"Oh, God," I breathe.

Salvatore's mouth covers mine. He licks at my lips, asking me to let his tongue inside.

I tighten my arms around his waist and pull him closer, opening for him happily.

Instead of kissing me, he whispers into my mouth, still playing with my nipples while I squirm against him. "Let him go, bella," he rasps in a soft plea.

The muscles in my back tighten as his voice and words and touch hit me all at once. I move my hands to the sides of his head. "I don't want him. I haven't wanted anyone else since the day I met you." I look him in the eyes as I say the words I've been confronting for months, holding them deep inside of myself.

His eyes widen and soften, and then he kisses me until I'm panting, rubbing my legs together and wet enough to leak down my inner thighs.

Salvatore pulls away, and I whimper again. "Wait."

I feel the ghost of his smile against my mouth briefly before he steps back, shoving his hands in his pockets, looking at me again. "Perfetto," he says.

I shiver. I was so goddamn close to coming. "Salvatore." It's my turn to beg.

He pulls a cell phone from his right pocket. He places it on the bathroom sink. "For you. There are two numbers saved on it."

I blink in a horny haze for a few seconds before I put two and two together. "Giulio and Alfonso?"

Salvatore nods, a proud smile on his face. "If you ever need anything and I'm...not here, you call them."

"You said you wouldn't be long."

He looks at me with the saddest eyes I've ever seen, bleaker than the day we met. I get what he's not saying faster this time. Nothing is guaranteed in his life. Nothing is safe. Not him, and for as long as I'm with him, certainly not me.

I nod, swallowing a lump of emotion.

His hand settles over my stomach, the tip of his

thumb brushing my mound. I cover his hand with mine. He kisses me softly on the lips and then turns away, exiting the bathroom. "Bella," he says, turning around in the doorway. "When I return," he says, looking me over from head to toe again. "I want to find you just like this."

I'm still shivering when I hear the front door close.

12 / *SALVATORE*

I leave Shae with half a dozen bodyguards who know that I'll rip them apart with my bare hands without a second thought if she's not safe and sound when I return.

I don't threaten my men often. I've always found it easier to inspire loyalty in good men by giving it in return, which means they all know that when I do threaten them, it is anything but idle. There are frivolous mistakes I can accept, worrying mistakes I will correct, serious mistakes that might lead to...retirement. That is our contract. But now, there is a new measure. If anything happens to Shae, I'll mete out a punishment they've never seen before.

I only climb into my car when I feel as if I've made my position crystal clear.

Lorenzo drives with Federico in the passenger seat. We maneuver through the city in relative silence, although every now and then, the sound of one of their aggravated grunts filters to me in the back seat, followed by a short argument about some turn Federico thinks Lorenzo should have taken or how fast — or slow — the car is moving.

Their bickering almost reminds me of Giulio and Alfonso, and it settles my nerves, easing the anxiety I feel about leaving Shae. It doesn't matter how many bodyguards I've left with her; I'll never feel that she's safe unless she's by my side, but that's an illusion. She's in more danger with me than ever, and at some point between yesterday afternoon and this morning, the goal shifted away from figuring out who's trying to kill me to something else I won't even allow myself to name just yet, not even in my mind.

But the closer we get to our destination, the sharper my purpose becomes.

Palermo is a tourist city, but the summer season is long over. In season, the streets are full of pedestrian tourists, making their way to and from the beach, dining on the sidewalks, shopping for mass-produced local knickknacks. It's easy to hide in that throng if necessary. It's one of the reasons I bought property here. In the off-season, it's so much harder to hide who you are, but I'm not looking to hide. While Lorenzo and Federico bicker, I pull in all of the best parts of me — the parts I've only ever shown to Shae — and hide them somewhere so far down inside myself that no one besides her will ever find them.

By the time we arrive at our destination, I have become myself again.

Tommaso rushes from his front door to meet my car.

He pulls my door open before Lorenzo can even push his foot down on the brake.

"Benvenuto, padrino," he says, lowering his eyes respectfully. "I'm honored."

I don't require this kind of deference, but I don't have time to mince words reminding him of that. I'm here on a mission.

I stand from the car and place my hand on his shoulder. It's late fall, but the wind from the water is still warm enough that I'm happy I didn't wear a coat. "You've done a good job of keeping this secret for me," I tell him. "Until now."

He grimaces, wiping at his shiny forehead as Lorenzo also stands from the car. I see the moment when he realizes that he's trapped between us.

"Do you have something to tell me?" I ask evenly.

He nods quickly. Nervously. I try not to put too much stock in the fear in his eyes. That could just as easily be intelligence as guilt; if I were him, I would be afraid of me as well.

Lorenzo moves his hand closer to the gun in his holster.

I glance quickly in his direction, telling him with just a look to wait.

There's always time to kill someone, but you can only do it once, so it's best not to pull the trigger — literally — until your enemy has given you all the information you need.

Assuming Tommaso is an enemy, of course.

"Only some of my men knew that I was hiding

anything. Even fewer knew what exactly or for whom. I've interviewed them all, but..." His voice gives out. His face has gone red, and he can't mop at the sweat pouring down it fast enough.

"You have a leak," I finish for him, "but you are still unsure exactly who it is."

Tommaso nods slowly. "No, b-but I am still investigating," he says, finally meeting my eyes. "I will find out who did this."

One of the things I've learned in my line of work is to trust myself enough to trust the people around me. It's a risk, but it's worth it, which is why I believe him.

"Okay."

Tommaso's eyebrows bunch together. "O...kay?"

"Okay. We will find the leak together."

Tommaso nods excitedly.

"But first, I need to see the package." Those words taste like dirt on my tongue.

* * *

"Figlio di putana!" Flavia spits out as soon as I descend into the cellar followed by a steady stream of curses against me, generations of my family, and God for making me.

When I sent her here, I told Alfonso to make sure she was comfortable, but not terribly so. I wish I hadn't been so charitable.

The cellar is spacious enough to fit a small metal cot in one corner, a small dresser, and then a toilet in another. There's no privacy, and the room is at least a few degrees cooler than the modern, renovated, spacious house Tommaso led me through. It's certainly well below her standards, but as prisons go, Flavia deserves worse.

I could waste my time wondering why I'd been so lenient, but it was Shae. It was always Shae.

I only have so much charity left.

I stop at the bottom of the steps and stare at her while she flings all manner of curses at me; none of them even touch me because I hate her. Also, she's shackled to the bed by her left ankle, and without all the expensive skincare and trips to her plastic surgeon, she looks like herself, and I know she hates that. Her clothes are clean but cheap. No makeup. No money. No influence. No way out of here unless I change my mind.

Knowing that she is completely at my mercy brings a smile to my face, so I stand at the foot of the stairs and let her curse me all she wants.

Federico moves around me into the room to place a chair for me to sit. "Padrino," he says formally. "Do you want me to stay?"

"No, I think my wife and I should catch up alone. Don't you agree?" I aim that question at her.

She narrows her eyes to menacing slits and finally shuts the fuck up.

"We'll be at the top of the stairs," he says.

I nod and walk toward her as Federico leaves, but then I stop and call him back. "Give me one of your guns," I say, extending my hand.

He nods and presses a pistol into my palm. It's heavy.

A little old-fashioned. Very effective. Giulio prepared him well.

I wait until Federico's steps have stopped echoing across the room before walking to the chair, picking it up by the back with one hand and bringing it much closer to Flavia.

"No need to stand," I tease because I cannot help the pleasure it gives me to see her in these circumstances.

She seethes as I sit and cross my legs. I don't rush, even though I refuse to spend any more time away from Shae than is strictly necessary.

I hold the gun casually in my right hand. Try as she might, Flavia's gaze keeps flitting to it, telegraphing her fear without meaning to.

Eventually, the familiarity of dim lighting and the heavy weight of a gun in my hand hit me, and I smile. "We've been here before," I announce with glee.

"What are you talking about?" she curses. "I would have rather died than step foot on this backward island."

That pulls a soft chuckle out of me. I've known her for over twenty years, and finally, Flavia has made me laugh. There's a first time for everything.

She spits on the floor at my feet. Or she tries to. I imagine she's far too dehydrated to spare the moisture.

"I meant we've been in this predicament before," I clarify. "When I first discovered how treacherous you can be."

"As if you're any better."

I shrug at the truth of her words. "I would never lie

about something so petty. I understand if you cannot say the same."

She rolls her eyes and looks away briefly before turning back. Her voice is as venomous as ever. "You won't kill me."

"No?" I ask in legitimate shock. I lean forward and lift my eyebrows. "And what makes you think that?" I've never been more interested in anything she has to say in all the years I've known her.

"You need me."

Oh. Apparently, that chuckle was a crack in the wall because those three words make me laugh until there are actual tears in my eyes.

The metal bed cries as she scrambles to the edge of it.

The laughter dies on my lips, and my grip tightens on the gun. I aim it directly at her chest.

She stops moving and lifts her hands in surrender. "I can help you is what I meant to say."

"How?"

"If you're here, that means—" She swallows slowly. "That means my contingency plan worked."

"Oh?"

"When I..." She stalls, hating to admit the depth of her complicity. Even now.

Her father would be so disappointed.

So, I help her. "When you contracted with your lover and the dregs of your family to try and kill me." I roll my hand to speed this confession along.

She balls her hands together in a tight fist. "Yes.

When I...did that, I knew there was a chance that I might fail."

"And you did." It's petty and maybe even counterproductive. I don't care.

"So, I-I sent a letter to a friend and told her that if I ever fell out of contact that she should put it in the post."

"What was in the letter?"

"Release me, and I will—"

I shift the gun to the left and shoot the stone wall. A dust cloud fills the air. Flavia flinches as debris rains down on her.

"I accused you of planning to make a move on Aldo Milanese's territory."

My jaw is tight with rage. "Who did you send it to?" I shift the gun back to her chest so she doesn't try to deal again. I was humoring her before. I'm not in the mood for that anymore.

"My father's aunt in Puglia," she admits, tears filling her eyes and falling down her face. So, she's not too dehydrated to weep. Shame.

"And to whom did you tell her to send the letter?" I ask, my brain already pulling the weaves of this new plot and its implications together.

She moves her hands out in front of her, palms pressed together as if in prayer. "Please. Please."

"Who?" I can guess, but I have so many enemies. There's no time to waste. Not with Shae here. Not when she is pregnant with my child.

"Aldo M-milanese." She stutters. "Please."

I lower the gun and let my eyes leave her sweaty, wet

face. I need to think through the possibilities and dangers. There are too many to count. It is so easy to ignore her begging and wailing to focus on the matter at hand. I try to imagine myself in Aldo's shoes. If I heard someone was trying to encroach on my territory, I know what I would do. But clearly, he and I are different men because I am still alive.

"Please, please, please," Flavia wails.

"Padrino?" Lorenzo calls down.

"What?"

"Are you well?"

"Pleasepleaseplease!"

"I'm fine."

The fingers on my free hand twitch, remembering the feeling of Shae's skin, as my brain tries to work through the information Flavia has given me.

"Pleasepleaseplease." Her pleading is giving me a headache.

Without looking, I lift the gun and pull the trigger twice. Flavia's pathetic whining stops. For good. I can finally think. This relief might be fleeting, but it is no less sweet.

"Everything is fine. Tell Tommaso there is some trash I need him to attend to."

"Si, padrino."

SOME MEN in my line of work — many, actually — feel sullied by what we do. Men who imagine that they — we — are better than we are. We are not, and I refuse to shrink away from culpability for the life I chose. I am exactly who I wanted to be.

I've made sacrifices for power. I've killed to gain it and keep it. I've killed to enrich someone else's bank account and my own. I've killed for revenge. I've killed to make an example.

But Flavia is the first time I've killed someone to set myself free. And I'd do it again. Not just because she's now out of my life but because it felt good.

When I ascend from the cellar, I feel like a brand-new man. I stop at the top stair and close my eyes, taking a deep breath in through my nose. I hold the crisp, fresh sea air in my lungs for a moment and then exhale the past two decades with my wife and all the obligations to her family that she represented.

"Padrino?" Lorenzo says carefully.

I hear him but from far away. I've wanted to be rid of Flavia since the moment I tethered the fate of my ambitions to her family name. I used to hope that one day she would disappear, but deep down, I always knew one of us would have to die, and I've fantasized about all the many ways I could kill her when I was ready — assuming she didn't kill me first. Not for lack of trying.

If I'm honest, I always assumed it would be my hands around her throat; something personal, intimate. She was my wife, after all.

And then I met Shae.

After twenty-two years, the most intimacy Flavia and I share at the end is the same air of a cool cellar and whatever infinitesimal drops of her blood on my clothes. That is all, and it's still more than she deserved.

I open my eyes with a smile, the memory of Shae's smiling face brightening even the darkest parts of my soul. I pass the gun into Lorenzo's waiting hands. "I'm ready."

Tommaso's house has a beautiful view of the sea. Lorenzo and Federico lead me out onto a balcony that wraps around his estate. They walk at a brisk pace, but I slow down, enjoying the way the lighter blue of the sky meets the darker blue of the water on the horizon.

I don't think I've ever done that before, just soaked in the beauty of a moment. Maybe with Shae. It all comes back to her.

"Padrino." I refuse to focus on that voice long enough to tie it to a name. My hand and jaw flex in something like irritation. I want to go home. I want to fall into the warmth of Shae's body. I want this to be over.

I turn to my men and nod, allowing them to lead me away.

Tommaso greets me on a large terrace. One of his men stands by, silent and not too close, not a threat. He and Tommaso hide their nerves well enough, but I can feel it, the terror that fills you when the devil you know is made flesh.

"Padrino," Tommaso says in greeting.

"I have a plan." My gaze flickers to the other man on the balcony.

Tommaso glances quickly behind him. "That is Carlo. I trust him above all others."

I nod slowly. "Then, if any of this gets out, I know who to kill."

Tommaso stiffens, but he nods. I look to Carlo, and he nods as well. We all know the risks.

I beckon him over with a friendly wave. His steps are jerky at first, but they get stronger, and I smile approvingly at Tommaso. "I will make sure to tell Giulio about you two."

They grin happily at one another briefly before the smile on my face falls.

"Here is my plan," I say gravely because this is the most serious thing I've ever done. Shae's life and the life we can build together depends on the plan I cobbled together hastily while the scent of gun smoke hung in the air.

After I've sketched out the broad strokes of my plan, the men scatter.

Lorenzo goes to retrieve the car. Federico offers to help Carlo dispose of Flavia's body. That leaves me alone on the terrace with Tommaso.

"Do you want anything to drink, padrino? Eat? Anything. My home is yours." His nerves have returned, and I suddenly feel weary. This is a part of the job I haven't managed to erase, not even with men like Alfonso and Giulio. It is tiresome to watch my men bow and scrape like peasants.

"I want for nothing," I tell him good-naturedly. "But I do have a job for you. Something no one can know."

His eyes widen in shock, and he nods, eagerly. "Anything," Tommaso whispers, his voice full of unnecessary reverence.

"I need you to send a message."

"Si, padrino. To who?"

I shake my head. "One to Molise. One to Abruzzo."

Somehow his eyes manage to widen even more as I tell him the message he must pass along.

Shae

I take my sweet time doing my hair, so I don't have a reason to get dressed, but putting my hair into Bantu knots only takes so long, so I kill some more time by hanging my clothes and Salvatore's in the closet. And then giving myself a tour of his apartment. Still naked as the day I was born.

Zoe always says there's no kind of freedom like walking around your home naked. But this is not my house, and I am not a bold person by nature, so I move around Salvatore's apartment on the balls of my feet, tentatively, slowly turning doorknobs, peeking into new rooms through cracked doors. I don't touch a thing.

I don't find anything out of the ordinary, but with Salvatore gone, I feel just how deeply I don't belong here or in his world.

But I don't want to live in his world; I just want him.

I came here for him.

I think I tried to ignore that at the time, but I can't now. I came here for Salvatore. Zahra found Giulio. Zoe can take care of herself. Neither of them needs me. We're not children anymore. And I only want Salvatore. And just as I think that, the front door opens, and I rush into the living room, forgetting that I'm naked. Maybe I've finally tapped into the freedom Zoe was talking about.

Lorenzo — I think, I can't really tell them apart — looks at me quickly and then away with wide eyes before Salvatore breezes into the room, smiling when he sees me. Lorenzo pulls the door closed quickly behind him.

I should feel embarrassed, but I don't. "You told me to be naked."

"I did." He starts to finger his beard, stroking the gray hair, watching me.

"So, I am."

He smiles and scratches under his chin. He lifts his eyebrows in interest. "You are."

"Are you done with...work?" I ask tentatively, naïvely.

His eyes lift to my face, and he smiles. "Si, bella. For now."

"Good." I shove my hands behind my back and cross one leg in front of the other, posing for him without thinking. No, *this* is the freedom Zoe promised.

I watch Salvatore's gaze move down my body again, his eyes squinting in focus, his hand caressing his beard, his tongue wetting his lips. There's nothing like the way he looks at me.

"Did you just want to watch me?" I ask, my heart racing a mile a minute.

"Not only that," he says, not making a move. "You're beautiful."

My stomach growls before I can respond appropriately.

Salvatore's eyes lift to mine, and there's anguish — actual anguish! — on his face.

"No," I whine.

"Si, bella. We will eat first."

"But I'm horny."

He walks toward me and pulls me into his arms.

I whimper and press my body shamelessly against him, wrapping my arms around his shoulders.

He kisses me deep and slow. He smiles against my mouth. Something feels different about this embrace. He feels looser, calmer in my arms, hungrier, and that feeds something primal inside me.

I'm just about to climb up into his arms when he slowly pushes me away, his teeth scraping along my bottom lip. "Let me feed you first, bella."

I whine like a spoiled child.

"And then, I will feast on you."

I shudder in his hold. "Okay, deal. But I'm not going to wait forever."

He holds my face in his hands. "Believe me, I would not be able to last that long."

I rub myself against him again, brushing his hardening erection with my stomach. "I don't know," I tease. "I believe in you."

I MAKE Shae lunch and then feast on her, exactly as I promised. And then she falls asleep in my arms. For a while, I hold her, enjoying her soft breaths on my neck and the calm I feel having her in my arms where I know she's safe.

I feel at ease.

I never thought I could have an afternoon like this. That's exactly what I thought the day we met. Instead of feeling gratitude for a day I couldn't imagine, like I did then, now every minute with her only makes me want more.

There's a knock on the front door.

I kiss Shae softly on the crown of her head. She moans lightly in her sleep, clutching at me as I carefully and reluctantly move her from my chest to the bed, adjusting the satin bonnet she pulled on before letting me throw her onto the mattress. I make sure her hair is covered before I climb to my feet and walk quietly to the door and turn around. Maybe one day I won't need to get one last look at her before I leave, but that day will be far into the future if it comes at all.

I find Federico on the other side of the door, looking serious and uncomfortable. "I'm sorry to interrupt, padrino."

I bat that deference away. "If I didn't want you to, then you would not have. What do you need?"

He relaxes. "Tommaso said he'll be at the club tonight. Everything is ready."

I look over my shoulder as if I can see Shae through the wall, asleep and naked in my bed. This was my idea, and I know — even now — that this is the only way, but there is a knot in my gut at what it will require of me.

Of what could happen to Shae if something goes wrong.

"Padrino," Federico starts carefully. I can guess what he's about to say, but I hold my hand in the air, stopping him from digging a hole I would prefer he not climb inside.

"Tell all the men to be ready at sundown." I turn back to him, eyes hard, voice steel. I don't need anyone thinking I'm weak. Shae has burrowed her way under my skin, but that opening — that softness — is only for her.

Federico's back straightens, and he nods quickly. "Si, padrino."

I close the door and return to Shae. The desire to strip my clothes off and crawl back into bed beside her, to wake her with my fingers rubbing her clit so her first conscious word will be to moan my name, is stronger than any urge I've ever known. I want to fast-forward to a day where nothing gets in the way of taking care of her. Where I can wake her with my mouth on her cunt, slide into her, make her beg for every hard stroke and thank me when she comes.

I can't do any of those things right now. I need to let her rest, and I need space to think about what is coming and prepare. But I watch her from the door for a few moments and smile when she flips onto her stomach and gathers my pillow greedily into her arms, rubbing her face against it while she snores softly. I watch her for a few seconds before I finally manage to tear myself away and close the door lightly.

There are two more bedrooms down the hall. One is a simple guest bedroom that I've never used besides the en suite bathroom this morning. I use the other room as an office. It's not as useful as my office in Naples, but not useless, by any means.

I close the door almost all the way but pull the curtains shut tight. There's a rug in the middle of the room, something very expensive I bought on a whim one day in Florence. Flavia had admired it in a store, and it made me happy to purchase it in front of her and then watch her waste weeks waiting excitedly for its arrival. When she finally realized that she would never see that rug again, the disappointment deflated her for a few hours at least. I, on the other hand, had smiled for days.

I have always believed in grabbing any amount of joy with both hands.

I bend over and grab a corner before pulling the

heavy thing out of the way. Dust lifts into the air. I sneeze and cough but feel assured, at least, that no one has been in this room besides me.

There's a square outline of a trapdoor in the wooden floor that holds my contingency plan.

One of many.

I kneel down and run my fingers along a floorboard, searching for the outline of the small button. When I locate it by feel, I press down, and the secret compartment in the floor opens on a spring. I dig the tips of my fingers into the small opening and pull the hatch, waiting for the stale air to clear.

There's a flashlight at the top of the pile that I grab and then switch on. The batteries are old, and the light flickers at first before steadying. I move the shaft of light around, confirming that everything looks as it should; each box stacked neatly one on top of the other in order by size, with the largest deep at the bottom. When I'm satisfied once again that everything is as it should be, I set the flashlight to the side and pull each box out carefully. The first and smallest I set on the desk, the others I place on the floor around the room.

When the hole is empty, I close it and move the rug back into place. If all goes well, I don't plan to need this hiding place or this apartment ever again.

I have a few hours before I need to wake Shae up and prepare her for me to leave again. I *could* rest. I probably *should* rest. But my mind always works best when my hands are moving.

My mind wanders to Shae again, and my fingers

twitch with need for a few tense moments. I've just about pulled myself together when the door squeaks and drifts slowly open.

I'm not surprised to find Shae standing there. I'm relieved, actually.

She's wearing a long shirt that just barely covers her pussy. She blinks up at me with tired, trusting eyes. "You weren't there."

Her voice is scratchy, dry, delicate, and it rips me to shreds. I wasn't there, and she came after me. What could be simpler than that? I let her go once — pushed her to leave — but clearly, I'm not the only one who won't let that happen again.

I don't know how she manages to dig right to the center of me with just a look and a few words, but this is the moment I decide to stop questioning it. "I'm sorry, bella."

She shrugs. "It's okay." Her eyes move around the room. "I just wanted to make sure you hadn't left...me."

I narrow my eyes in her direction. "I would not."

She swallows and nods, her eyes going soft as she leans against the doorframe. "Do you...want to be alone? I can wait for you."

"No." I have guarded the boxes in this room for over twenty years, hiding these parts of myself from everyone. But not Shae. I extend my hand to her. "Come, bella. There are some things I need to show you."

There is a part of my brain so small that I know it cannot survive much longer. It wants Shae to run away. It wants her to close the door and distance herself from me.

It screams now from its small place, telling her to run as fast as she can. I hold my breath and watch her look around the room, considering. She sighs lightly then steps forward slowly, carefully navigating her way around the boxes on her toes, elongating her lovely bare legs.

She grabs my hand when she's close, and our fingers entwine. She presses herself against my side, and then we sink to the floor together.

She crosses her legs and rocks side to side, trying to get comfortable and hide her nakedness. I laugh and pull her into my lap. "Better?"

"Harder," she mumbles, rolling her hips against my cock.

I laugh again and kiss her neck.

"What...what is all this?"

"Many things. Important things."

"Okay, thanks. That's a very helpful answer."

I kiss along her jaw and then reach for the closest box to me. I open it to show Shae the Beretta I haven't used in years. She gasps before catching herself and pressing her mouth closed.

"This was my father's," I tell her. The gun is old. It needs to be cleaned. I know I have a box of cleaning materials in the bottom shelf of the desk, but I don't keep this gun to use. It's sentimental, and I try to find the words to describe that to Shae, knowing that she's lived such a different life from mine.

While I try to collect my thoughts, Shae reaches for the gun with a long finger but stops and asks me silently for permission.

"It's okay," I tell her, holding her close.

It takes a few seconds before her hand moves again, shaking. Her fingertips brush along the barrel. "I've never —" She gulps. "I've never touched a gun before."

I kiss her arm. "My father had a gun on him at all times. He used to say that a man needed an army." She goes stiff in my arms. "Or he needed to *be* an army. I've lived by those words since I was a boy."

She cups my cheek with one warm palm and shakes her head. "That doesn't sound like the kind of motto a kid should adopt."

"Probably not," I agree. "But I grew up in this world. My father was an enforcer for a capo in Rome. Even before I realized who he was, I knew. He used to come to us covered in sweat and blood, with flowers for my mother and a present for me. He'd stay for a few days, sometimes more, and then leave."

"For...work?"

"And to be with his other family."

"Oh," she whispers, pained.

"He wasn't a great man, but he was a provider. We never went hungry or cold. My mother never had to leave the house to work. She could devote herself entirely to taking care of me, whether I wanted to be babied or not."

It's been years since I've thought about my mother and even longer since I've spoken of her to anyone. I haven't ever trusted another person — not even Giulio or Alfonso — with such intimate details of my past. Being able to do that with Shae feels like a weight I've been carrying on my back for decades is dissolving.

"She kept an immaculate home," I tell Shae with a smile. "But she was not the best cook."

"So, you cooked?" Shae laughs.

"Yes. At first, I just wanted to help her not burn dinner." She giggles and squirms against me. "But then I realized that I enjoyed it."

"That's adorable." Her hand caresses my cheek, and I close my eyes to enjoy her touch and her weight on me, hearing her soft breaths.

"I want you to understand the kind of family I come from, so this next part will make sense."

She kisses the space between my eyes and whispers, "okay," against my skin.

"Even though I grew up in this world, it didn't touch me at first. I didn't understand exactly who my father was or the kind of family he came from until much later. That's why when I was a boy, my happiest moments came in the summer when my uncles came to Rome."

"How many uncles?"

"Three. But we only ever saw them once a year."

"Why?"

"Because they didn't live in Italy. One lived in Brazil, one in Australia, and the other in America."

"You have family in America?" She perks up with excitement. I hoped she would.

I nod. "Daniele. He was my favorite uncle, and he always brought his son, Dante, with him. He was my favorite cousin."

"Yeah?"

I nod again. "My other uncles would come for a few

weeks and then return home to their families, but Daniele and Dante would stay the entire summer. I thought it was because Daniele missed home, and maybe he did, but later I realized it was because he and my father had their own..." I shrug, trying to find the right word for their business endeavors, illegal as they were.

"They were criming," Shae says nonchalantly, still caressing me. "I got it."

I cannot help but laugh. "Yes. But I didn't know that then. All I knew was that each summer, Daniele and Dante would arrive with gifts from America. My mother would try to make all of Dante's favorite Italian foods — which were thankfully my favorite foods, so I could fix her mistakes. Every summer, he and I would be thick as thieves. I helped him with his Italian, and he returned the favor with my English."

"I love that." Her eyes have gone soft with emotion. I imagine tears might not be far off.

"Those summers were the happiest of my life before I met you."

Shae's smile falters. "What...what happened?"

For the first time in so long, I don't swallow the pain and all the accompanying sadness. "My mother told me that my father wanted to leave the business. Maybe. I don't know. I might never know. All I remember is that one day in the autumn, he left home and never returned. A few months later, we heard that my uncle in Australia had died in a car accident. My uncle in Brazil had a heart attack a month later, they said."

Shae grabs my face with both hands, her eyes shining with tears.

I smile at her as best I can. "Daniele lasted ten more years, but every time he contacted my mother and I with a few dollars to help us get by, he was in a different place."

"He was on the run?"

I nod.

"I never saw any of my cousins again after that, not even Dante. I was too busy helping my mother make rent."

"How did you...sign up? Why would you?"

I shrug. "It's the family business. This is what I know. My father's reputation was ruined, but he still had friends who left us groceries when we needed them and gave me a little work here and there."

"But...but what if...?"

"What if I've worked with the men who killed my father and uncles?"

She nods slowly.

"I have, actually, but not in many years."

"How do you know for sure?"

My smile — like my soul — feels hollow, the way I felt before I met her. "Because I killed almost everyone who was involved in my father's death. I took their lives and their territories. I made sure they paid me back in blood and power for what they took from us."

"I don't want that for our baby," she whispers quietly.

I wrap my arms around her waist. "Neither do I, bella. That's why I have to do this."

I can see the question she wants to ask. If she does, I'll tell her. I know that as sure as anything else. But she doesn't speak, so I reach for another box on the floor and place it on her lap. "Open it."

Her hand is hesitant again, but when she lifts the lid up, I feel her exhale at the stack of papers. "What's this?"

"My birth certificate. A family tree going back over a century." I move the papers to one side and grab a book at the bottom. "This has the information to all of my international bank accounts."

"I don't—"

"Yes, bella, you do. My father never got the chance to provide for my mother. Or maybe he didn't have the foresight. I won't make that mistake." She's shaking like a leaf in my arms. I hold her close, but I don't stop. There might not be time to do this again. "My father was a flawed man, but he was right about one thing. If anything happens to me, you find Giulio, Alfonso, Lorenzo, or Federico because I do have an army, and if anything happens to me, they will take care of you and our child."

"How do you feel?" Salvatore asks while I close my eyes, chew, and dance in my seat. His voice is a melodic mixture of concern and happiness, warm, gentle.

"Amazing," I say before shoveling another forkful of the best seafood pasta I've ever had into my mouth. So far, I haven't eaten a meal that Salvatore hasn't cooked for me. His cooking is as good as his dick. So, if the plan was to seduce me with orgasms and pasta, it's working. To be honest, I would have settled for far less. But that's the thing about Salvatore, I think, he's never let me settle once.

I want to thank him for this dinner and his care and his dick, but that will have to come later. Right now, I'm too busy spearing a piece of lobster onto my fork. I groan when I take that next bite.

Salvatore's eyes crinkle at the corners when he smiles, and his lips practically disappear behind his facial hair. He's going to be the biggest pushover as a father, I think out of nowhere, twirling some linguine onto my fork.

"What is that smile for?" he asks casually, reaching for his glass of water. He takes a sip, watching me with light dancing in his eyes.

I chew my food and swallow. "No reason. I'm just...happy."

He grabs my thigh and squeezes. "Good. You deserve that."

"You've been telling me that since we met."

"You are stubborn," he says. "You didn't believe me the first time. But you do now?" He lifts an eyebrow at me.

I nod and stare him down. "I do. And I deserve you, too. You know that now, right?" I'm ready for his objections.

He squeezes my leg again. "I do."

I use more food to hide my smile while Salvatore sits back in his chair and crosses his legs.

"Do you need to rest?"

That question stops the fork halfway to my open mouth. "Why?" I ask, my sex already clenching. "What did you...have in mind?"

Those crinkles deepen into creases that soon enough will be there permanently, and I want that. I want to make sure his laugh lines are mine. "Not that for once."

I bite back a frown. "Oh."

"I have to go out for...business," he says carefully. "I thought you might be tired. You can stay here and rest tonight. There's a spa in this building and—"

"No, thanks. I'll come with you," I say, turning back to my pasta. I grab a hunk of bread I would seriously consider dating if I weren't all in on this be-with-my-baby-daddy plan. I dip it into the sauce and close my eyes while I bite. "Amazing," I mumble with a full mouth.

Salvatore's voice is soft. I hear him shifting uncomfortably in his seat. "It could be...dangerous."

"Probably," I agree, snagging a piece of octopus, coating it in the sauce, and smearing it onto the last of the bread in my other hand before shoving the whole thing into my mouth.

"I want you to be safe."

I nod and chew. "Me too," I mumble behind my hand. "I definitely didn't come here to get shot or anything."

His hand is back on my thigh. "I don't know what might happen tonight, bella. You would be safer here."

I imagine lots of things could happen. *Anything* could happen when the father of your child is apparently in the mafia, so I guess he'll just have to keep his promise to me and be my army. Sounds legit to me. But my mouth is too full to state the obvious, so I just keep nodding at him.

Salvatore shifts closer. He takes a slow, loud, deep breath in. He presses his forehead to my shoulder and exhales as his arms wrap around my waist. He sounds so goddamn weary that it breaks my heart. I swallow the food in my mouth and tilt my head to rest on top of his. His hair smells like sea salt. It's my turn to take a slow, deep breath.

"What do you need to do?" I ask softly.

"I think I know who's trying to kill me."

"Is that what you were doing when you left this morning?"

"Yes."

"Who is it?"

"Another member of my...organization."

"Why?"

He squeezes me again. "My wife set me up."

My heart freezes at those words. To be honest, I'd completely forgotten about his wife. I don't know her, so I can't hate her, but if he's right, and she's the reason someone is trying to kill him, I'll learn how to hate her on my baby's behalf.

"Why did she—"

"We hated one another. Deeply."

"Hated?" My heart is racing.

"Bella."

"Tell me."

"She's dead. I killed her."

"To-today?"

"Yes."

"And then you came back to me?"

"Always."

My mother always said you never really know yourself until you end up at a crossroads in life. I'd thought after years of unhappiness and boredom with Steve that I was a coward. How else to explain wasting so much of my time? And maybe that was actually who I was then, but not anymore. I've spent just a few days with Salvatore, and each one has been a crossroads, and each time, I have chosen him.

The day we met, I discovered that I was a woman who would cheat without barely a second thought. I would throw years away for a bit of time with Salvatore, and I wouldn't regret it. I would spend months wanting to do it again.

I would abandon rescuing my cousin to stay by his side. I would let him whisk me away from everyone I know and love. And while Salvatore is holding me, admitting to murder — certainly not his first — I would accept it. And I would remember that after he committed that murder, he came home, fed me, and made me scream his name until my throat was sore. Because I accept him for who he is. This is the man I love, flaws and all.

Also, I would feel a small, messy, terrible bit of triumph because now, he's all mine. This is who I am, flaws and all.

"Okay," I breathe, rubbing my cheek into his soft hair, glancing at the rest of my pasta, which I hope I get to eat.

Salvatore pulls away and looks at me. "That is all you have to say? Okay?"

I shrug. "I was wondering what we were going to do about your wife, and now..." I shrug again. "So, what's next? Oh, is that why you need to go out tonight?"

His eyes are full of shock. "Yes. I think I know how to finish this."

"You don't sound happy about that."

He moves his hands under the hem of my shirt. One

palm covers my stomach; the other rests in the middle of my back. His touch makes me shiver.

"The easiest way to finish this is to force the issue. I need to meet whatever is coming head-on."

"Oh. That's smart."

He laughs softly. "I'm glad you approve because if you come tonight, you will be a part of this."

"How?"

Salvatore sighs. "I married my wife because her father used to be a very powerful man. He's been dead for many years, but there are many people who are still very loyal to her because of him."

"Oh!" I gasp. "I'm guessing those same people would definitely hate it if you disrespected your wife by showing up with your new younger, prettier Black *and* American lover."

He nods. "I need one of her allies in particular to come out in the open. But I can do this without you. There are many reasons for people to hate me, especially anyone loyal to her."

"I believe that," I say with a smile that tugs one from him in return. "But if you want to press the issue..." I lift my eyebrows to check in with him.

"I do."

"Then I give you permission to use me."

He growls and takes my mouth. I never eat the rest of my dinner, but Salvatore promises to make it for me again when this is all over. And I plan to hold him to that.

"I don't know about this." I've been staring at my reflection in the mirror while Salvatore helps me dress without an ounce of urgency in his movements. His fingers dig into my waist, brush my nipples, and tease the hair at the nape of my neck, none of which is necessary to help me wiggle into the tight black dress that appeared out of nowhere before we'd even finished cleaning up the kitchen.

"I do," Salvatore says, taking his sweet time zipping me into this dress, the pads of his fingers smoothing the way of the metal clasp.

"This dress is..." I want to say 'a lot,' but it's actually very little.

While I was worried about whether or not I had something fancy enough to wear out — I did not — Salvatore was apparently sending his armed and terrifying bodyguards out to buy the shortest, tightest dress they could find.

"How did they even know what size dress I'd need?"

His hands grip my waist as he kisses a path across my upper back until his face appears over my shoulder. His gaze, much like my skin and pussy, is on fire. "I know your body," he whispers before licking my ear.

"Do we have time?"

"No," he laughs, darting away.

I'm disoriented for a few seconds at the loss of his touch. "But..." I whine, following him into the bedroom, pulling at the waves from my Bantu knots. My hair's still a little damp, but in this dress, no one will be looking at my hair.

He laughs and pulls on his suit coat. He looks dangerous in all black, and that does nothing to dampen my lust for him.

But I do have to wonder how the fuck I missed this sophisticated and deadly air about him when we met. That's when I realize that he's not wearing his eyeglasses tonight, and I see it — the disguise he was wearing that first day. I tilt my head, picturing him in that damn apron — the one I'd more than once imagined wearing while serving him a meal that I certainly did not cook while tossing and turning on that lumpy ass couch. I guess those innocent ornaments — his apron and glasses — fooled me, but not anymore, maybe not at all. Because even now, I can still see him as a version of the kindly, older restauranteur who turned me out with an afternoon of gastronomic foreplay, civilized conversation, and risky sex. Except now I know what I didn't know then, no matter how he presents.

I also know for sure that Salvatore was always supposed to be mine.

"Are you ready?" he asks, offering me his hand.

There's no hesitation, and I rush to his side in heels that are a little taller than I'm used to, but make my legs look amazing.

WE DRIVE WEST ALONG the coast to a popular nightclub famous for its strong drinks and a dance floor that spills onto the beach. It's aimed at tourists, and the cover charge and drink prices reflect that. So do the big security guards giving the women in short, tight dresses far more attention than me or my men. Shae has to squeeze my hand when the bouncer asks her cleavage for identification to keep me in line.

Under normal circumstances, I would never be caught dead in a place like this, but this club is the perfect setting for an illicit business deal. So I swallow the affront to Shae's honor, knowing that it will make me more dangerous in the long run. There might be holes in my plan that I don't have time to fill, but I'm more than prepared to shoot my way through them.

This is not the way I do business normally. I hate putting myself or my men in danger, and I've taken someone out for doing that before. So, I'm galled to have put not just my men and myself but Shae and our baby in a situation where I can't control any of the variables. I don't even have Giulio and Alfonso by my side.

But Shae's warm hand in mine gives me a clarity of purpose. I will do whatever it takes to end this quickly, *especially* if it means protecting my heart.

Lorenzo and Federico lead us toward a table in the middle of the room, where everyone can see us.

Shae presses herself against my back, her mouth bumping my ear as she leans close. "Um, is this okay?"

I stop at the table. Federico pulls a chair out for her. I squeeze her hand and brush my fingers along the side of her neck. "Do you trust me, bella?"

Her big doll eyes are wide, open pools of dark brown. "Yes," she says without hesitation.

I lean forward and brush my mouth across hers. I just want a small sip of her, the taste of her breath, but as soon as she opens her mouth, her tongue touches my lips, and then my hand is gripping the back of her neck, and our tongues are sliding together. I give myself over to this kiss. I give myself to Shae publicly, shamelessly. I'm not prepared when she pulls away.

There's a smile on her face, and she winks at me. "Gotta put on a show."

Laughter is easier in her presence. I smile lovingly at her, brushing my thumb over her soft jawline. "You might be very good at this."

"We'll see."

I turn and nod at Federico, and he moves away. I hold Shae's hand as she sits before taking my seat next to her.

I have Lorenzo grab the first waiter he sees to order a bottle of champagne. My hand is already on Shae's thigh, so I squeeze her when she jerks, reminding her that this is all for show. But what isn't a façade is when I pull her chair closer to mine, and she leans into me unconsciously, while her eyes roam around the room, taking everything in.

The dining area is elevated, giving us a great view of the dance floor below. At the edge of the building the tiled floor leads onto a sandy expanse and at the outer edges we can just glimpse the shimmering darkness of the sea beyond.

"What's this place called?" Shae asks.

"Shore."

She frowns at me. "That's so boring."

I hear one of my men snicker. "Si, bella. The padrino—"

She cuts me off with a raised hand. "Are you not the boss?" She turns fully toward me and squints, placing her hand lovingly on my chest. "I thought you were the boss."

"Do you want to be with the boss, my love?"

She presses her breasts against me, a wicked smile blessing her full mouth. "Yes." Shae is a beautiful and delicate contradiction. Her eyes are open and playful, maybe even innocent, but her voice is deep, sexy, demanding. Watching her blossom into herself will be a pleasure.

"I'm the boss of Naples," I tell her. My throat is dry, hoarse with need. "There's a boss of Sicily."

"All of Sicily?"

"It's complicated."

"So, he's your boss?"

"No," I say with a little too much emphasis, and she smiles, knowing she got me.

"Explain it to me, please." She whispers that request in the same tone of voice she used when she asked me to suck on her clit after lunch.

I grab the hand on my chest and lift it to my mouth, kissing each of her knuckles reverently. "Anything for you, bella." It's so easy to imagine a future just like this. Well, without the imminent danger, of course. "There are a number of Sicilian padrini, but the Palermo capo is the head of them all."

"Why?"

"This is the capital."

She nods, accepting that well enough. "But he's not your boss?"

"No."

"Who is?"

That, too, is complicated and best left to a more secure location. I kiss her hand again. "I can't tell you that right now. Later," I whisper against her skin.

"Okay," she says, nodding quickly and scooting closer. "Is there something specific you think I should do?"

I pull her closer, kissing her hard and fast, shocking a smile from her. She recovers quickly, kissing me back with the same eager fire as every other time our mouths have touched.

"Keep your eyes open and do exactly as I say," I whisper against her mouth.

"I can't wait to sit on your dick when we get back home."

***

Shae

I adore the sound of Salvatore's laughter. It's hearty and rich, and it makes all of my hair follicles shiver with excitement. I don't enjoy that he seems shocked by his own laughter as if he hasn't laughed or smiled or rested in years.

But he does with me, and that is something beyond words.

While he splutters, I resume scoping out the nightclub. It's as basic as its name. Zoe would call this place trashy-fancy, and she would hate it. Zahra would love it.

I'm undecided, but what I think of this place doesn't matter. We're here to do a job and get out — I think. I'm talking a big, brave game to Salvatore, but I'm quaking inside, to be honest.

But if this is what I have to do to make sure that my baby has a father, I'll do it. How very mafia wife of me!

Salvatore snakes an arm around the back of my chair and gently massages my neck.

My eyes begin to droop, and my head lolls forward. "That's...not...fair," I moan, his fingers working muscles I hadn't even realized were tense.

He chuckles but doesn't stop.

This has to be bad for the mission, right? How can I keep my eyes open — literally — with him touching me like this? Me and my hormones are already walking a tight rope, and the quick kisses, the touching, and all the laughter is too much. I mean, some of this might have been my fault, but that's really not the point. The point is that it's been barely two hours since he was inside me, and I still feel starved for him as if we've been separated for years.

Whatever the fuck is going on at this club needs to end soon. I'm horny.

"Please." The word slips out on a moan.

I'm not even sure he heard me at first, but then he uncrosses his legs, shifting closer to me. As soon as I feel his beard tickling my chin, I open my mouth eagerly, and he licks inside, searching for my tongue. I reach for him and wrap my arms around his neck as the sounds of the club fall away.

Nothing else matters besides Salvatore's lips and tongue, his grip on my neck, and the feeling of his hand snaking between my thighs.

This is definitely bad for whatever mission he's on, but I spread my legs for him because all this dangerous shit is barely my business. I'm just here to...

"Fuck," I grunt into Salvatore's mouth when his fingers slip inside my underwear and then my pussy.

His fingers and mouth are patient, stroking inside me slow as ever as if we're not in the middle of a club surrounded by his men or he's not trying to lure whoever tried to kill him out into the open. Salvatore fingers me as if we're back in his apartment without a care in the world; as if we have time for one orgasm after another.

Soon enough, I'm just moaning against his smiling mouth and trembling in his arms.

He stops abruptly, and I whimper against him shamelessly.

"Later," he whispers.

"You shouldn't have started something you weren't going to finish," I groan.

"I will finish it," he says, gripping my inner thigh, his wet fingers digging into my skin. "I promise."

It takes a few moments for me to pull myself back together. I'm hot, skin flushed, and all of a sudden happy that this dress is so thin and short because now that Salvatore's not kissing and fucking me, I start to cool down after a while. I have to blink a few times to focus on the club again. "Okay, so what should I be...doing?" I ask, still a little winded.

"You are doing it," he says breezily, crossing his legs at the knee and leaning into me, his hands still all over me, exactly as I like.

"You just want me to sit here and look cute?"

"Beautiful," he corrects me with a nod. "And yes."

I grin at him. "I finally found my talent. My mother will be so happy. Now I just need to figure out how to turn this into a career."

He squeezes my thigh again. "When this is over, you can do whatever you want. I'll make sure of that."

Well, all that cooling down is out of the window. I

squeeze my thighs together with his hand between them and squirm in my chair. If it were up to me, I think I might have crawled into his lap by now and more, which is a wild thought because I am *not* an exhibitionist. That's more Zoe's style. But with Salvatore... I think there are lots of things I'd be willing to try just to sate my desire for him.

But not right now. Since I'm here to be beautiful and put on a show, I channel every drop of courage I didn't know I had before this trip and lean into Salvatore's side. I look up at him and smile.

"What if I just want to be yours and have your babies?"

The light is low here, but not low enough that I don't see the fire in his eyes at my question. He nudges my legs open again and pushes his hand further between my thighs.

I cry out loud enough that all the tables nearby can hear me and a few of his men even flinch, almost turning to see what's going on, before they catch themselves. I don't care who hears me or sees us.

I'm wet, and Salvatore takes full advantage. He explores my slippery lips with his fingers, teases my opening, and then settles in to rub slow circles around my clit.

"Is that what you want, bella? To give me more babies?"

I lick his bottom lip while he's speaks, circling my hips around his hand. "I want you inside of me," I beg.

"Tell me," he demands, moving his ring finger into my opening. "Tell me you want the same future I do, and I'll give you whatever you want. I'll give you everything."

Those words make me shiver. "When you're not coming down my throat, I want you in my pussy. I want as many babies as we can handle and maybe one or two more."

He latches his mouth over mine to muffle the sound of my scream when he shoves two fingers deep inside me and strokes my clit with his thumb. He's been playing with me since before we left the apartment, so it doesn't take long for me to shudder through a sharp orgasm that takes my breath away. It's not the hardest orgasm of my life, but it leaves my legs shaking and my thighs sticky all the same.

And best of all, Salvatore holds me until I stop screaming and leaking around his fingers, making me promises with his hands and in Italian — even though I have no idea what he's saying — about the future we can build together.

I want that more than anything.

His eyes dart to my left, and whatever he sees there makes him pull away.

He squeezes my thigh with his wet hand. "Good girl," he whispers, kissing the corner of my mouth.

Those two words sound as obscene as letting him finger me in a nightclub, but I'm definitely beyond caring what anyone else thinks. I'm into it, and that's all that matters.

"Salvo!" someone calls in a harsh tone that absolutely ruins my post-orgasmic bliss.

I turn to see a man younger than him, but not by much, I'm assuming by the gray at his temple. He's standing on the other side of the table, glaring at Salvatore.

I scowl back at him. I'm not a violent person, but I could punch him based on his interruption and the way he's looking at my man. I don't like him one bit, but Salvatore has bodyguards to protect him, I guess. I'm just here to look beautiful, so I turn toward Salvatore, wondering what he thinks of this man, just in case I'm being ridiculous.

Speaking of obscene...

Salvatore has brought his fingers to his mouth. I can see my wetness on his digits under the scant light just before he sucks the taste of me from each of his fingers, slowly and deliberately. He savors the taste of my pussy while watching the other man with a deadly glare in his eye.

These hormones are fucking me all the way up because I'm horny all over again.

I think Zoe would call me trashy-fancy right now as well.

Luca Giordano normally never does his own dirty work. It's one of the many reasons why I can't respect him.

He's also loyal to Flavia's family, no matter that everyone knew the old man thought he was a Neanderthal, and Flavia agreed with her father. Luca was loyal to a fault. After the father's death, Luca's allegiances naturally shifted to the daughter. I used to harbor some hope that I could win him over to my side because a man who would be that loyal to someone who didn't think of him at all was an asset for someone like me. But Luca had more loyalty than sense, and that was not a boon. Some dogs only ever listened to one master, and it was kinder to put them down together.

I might have to eliminate Luca eventually, but for now, he could still be useful to me if I play him correctly. I worried it would take days to draw him out of hiding because he's too much of a coward to meet me face-to-face, but Shae was right; the offense to Flavia was enough to remind this coward of his spine.

Pathetic.

I gesture to Lorenzo to let Luca through with the hand that was just inside of Shae. The taste of her is making my blood boil, and since I can't fuck her right now, I decide to channel my lust into rage.

"You should be ashamed of yourself!" Luca yells, rushing toward the table, his face red and sweaty, his eyes wild with emotion he can't even muster in his own defense.

"I don't believe in shame. And considering the life you've lived, you'd be better off abandoning that emotion as well."

He blusters at that, spittle flying from his mouth. Shae shrinks away from him and grunts low in her throat in disgust.

"We are supposed to be men of honor," he finally manages to splutter at me.

I could laugh. Or yawn. "All those old lies simply ease the consciences of fools and children. Which one are you?"

Luca's fists are clenched at his sides. He doesn't know it, but this is why Flavia's father didn't respect him. The old man believed that a man who could not hold his temper was untrustworthy. I don't tend to agree. I think a man who can't control his anger can be useful if handled correctly, but he and Flavia were so busy sticking up their noses at men like Luca that they couldn't see his potential, while Luca was too lovesick to see how much Flavia despised him.

I cannot believe that I wasted years moving this empty chess piece around the board, and for what?

Shae leans into my side, one of her small hands resting on my chest lovingly. While Luca works himself into a frenzy, I take a deep breath and center myself.

I've always known that I was taking control of my world for some greater purpose than my own ego, but I was never sure exactly for what. Now, I know.

Shae. Our child. Our future.

Luca curses me, and I reach for the gun at my back.

Clarity. Purpose. Shae.

"What do you want, Luca?" I say, sounding bored even though I'm raging inside.

He had been speaking in Italian, but he switches to English now. For dramatic effect, obviously. "Where is your wife?" He spits that question, not at me but Shae, with such vehemence that my hand tightens around the butt of my gun.

I feel her blanch at that question, or maybe his tone of voice, even though she knows there is no reason to worry about Flavia ever again. "Look at me," I say in a voice betraying my anger.

Luca turns to me with a triumphant look.

I enjoy watching the pleasure on his face fade. "If the next words out of your mouth aren't an apology, I promise they will be your last." If nothing else, I know Luca understands that I do not make idle threats.

"Mi scuso," he spits at Shae.

"In English."

"I apologize."

"Now, don't ever even look in her direction again."

When he turns back to me, his face is the deepest shade of crimson and pouring with sweat. "You don't deserve her." He says this in English as well, hoping to wound her.

I look at Shae and smile.

Her eyes are nervously bouncing between Luca and me. She's fidgeting with my shirt, and I take my arm from her shoulder to grasp one of her hands and press it to my mouth. "I know."

She bites her bottom lip, nervous to smile in front of Luca.

"I meant your wife, you pig!" he barks.

I frown in confusion for a few seconds before giving Luca my attention again. "I don't deserve *Flavia?*" I ask in disbelief.

"She is a beautiful, classy woman who deserves loyalty, especially from her husband." He spits out that last word, years of bitterness barely leashed.

I laugh so hard there are tears in my eyes.

Shae tenses beside me, unsure of what's happening. I hate to leave her in confusion, but this situation is so ridiculous that I can't stop the laughter.

"Beautiful. Classy. Loyalty." I laugh between each word. "Spoken like someone who has never known her at all. Flavia? Beautiful? She'd better be. Do you know how much money she's wasted on plastic surgery? Classy?" I spit out that last word, beginning to sober and leash my anger again. "You can dress a goat in Gucci all you want. It will remain a goat. And Flavia wouldn't know how to spell the word 'loyalty' even if the answer could be found in the pants of those barely legal boys she was seducing all over Naples behind my back. As if I cared."

Luca looks on the verge of a heart attack, so I make sure to drive this knife deep before I twist it.

"Oh, did you think she's spent the last twenty years being faithful to me? Oh, no," I say, clucking my tongue like an old woman. "No, no, no, no, no. Trust me, she spent every day of our marriage fucking anyone with a dick and the whisper of facial hair. But for the last few years, she's used her...talents trying to convince them to kill me. While *you* were here all along. And yet she never even looked in your direction. I guess," I say, with a casual shrug, "it seems she wasn't willing to let the southern goatfucker touch her, even if you would have happily promised her my head on a spike. That's what she called you. I assume you know that, but just in case you were not aware. How do the ashes of your loyalty taste?"

I've been waiting years to say that, and it feels good. It feels even better when Shae rests her head on my shoulder, cuddling up next to me to drive the full offense of the years Luca waited for Flavia home.

She is perfect.

Luca's entire body is shaking with rage. If he were anyone else, I might have mustered an ounce of fear to see him in this state. If he were me, my gun would already be smoking. But Luca is Luca; no one can be someone they are not. Right before my eyes, his fists unclench, his jaw loosens, and his body sags forward. He becomes the man I always knew him to be.

"Patetico. Go away," I say, letting go of my gun so I can shoo him away like a child. "You're ruining my evening. You can flog yourself and jack off to memories of Flavia at some other table."

Shae squeaks and covers her mouth, laughing against my side, her body shaking with gentle tremors. I soften against her.

"We need to talk," Luca says in a quiet, defeated whimper.

"We've talked. I'm done."

"I don't believe that. You didn't bring..." He stops speaking abruptly.

I lift my eyebrows, waiting.

His eyes dart to Shae quickly and then back to me. Whatever he was about to say, I'll never know. Just like he'll never know how many bullets I can put in his body before the deejay recognize my gun firing over the bass of his music.

"We both know you didn't come to my establishment by accident. I assume you want me to send The Board a message. If so, let us get this over with."

I stare at him for a few tense moments. Luca is correct, but I don't want to make any of this easy on him, so I take a few seconds to indulge my ego.

When I turn to Shae, she's already shaking her head and grabbing at my shirt frantically.

I smooth my thumb over the high point of her left

cheek just to feel her. "Lorenzo is going to take you home."

"No," she breathes softly.

"Yes. I will be right behind you."

Her fingernails dig into my wrist, and I welcome even this pain. Any moment with Shae feels too good to be true.

"You did so well tonight. Let me finish what we started, and then I will be *right* behind you. I promise."

I hear Luca scoff, but it is quickly followed by the sound of Federico's gun cocking and Luca's whimpering wail.

I grab Shae's chin between two fingers and hold her gaze. There are things I want to tell her to soothe her mind, but not here, not now. But I look her deep in the eyes and try to silently communicate that I would never make a promise that I do not intend to keep.

Thankfully, I see the moment Shae understands — or at least acquiesces to my plea. "Fine. But remember what you promised to do when you get home."

I brush her mouth with mine. "How could I forget when you are always on my mind?"

Before I know what is happening, Shae has thrown herself into my arms and straddled my lap, pulling a surprised peal of laughter from my lips. The taste of her pussy is still on my tongue, and she licks it with relish while grinding her ass against my cock.

"Don't make me wait too long," she gasps against my mouth.

"Mai. Never."

She kisses me quickly and then crawls from my lap with a smile on her face. She wiggles her soft body to right her dress, and I watch her in awe.

"Don't get undressed," I command. She nods eagerly. "Lorenzo, take her home."

"Si, padrino."

I caress my lips, the taste of her still fresh there, and watch as Lorenzo leads my heart and soul from the building. I hate to be separated from them, but with those vital organs gone, I can do what needs to be done without qualms.

Once they disappear from view, I stand from my chair and lock hard eyes with Luca. "Lead the way."

I TAKE my gun from my holster in the middle of the dance floor. It would be polite to wait, but no one has ever accused me of being polite. Not even Shae.

There's a black door at the far end of the club, and it blends in almost seamlessly with the wall. If Luca hadn't been heading right for it, I would have missed it completely, but there's no time to panic about all the things I don't know. This particular danger has come and gone, and there are new worries to occupy my mind. There's always more danger on the horizon. That's why I'm here.

Luca takes a keyring from his pocket. I wait impatiently while he unlocks the door in full view of the club and pulls it open. The light from the hallway inside illuminates a patch of the dance floor before spilling onto the sand. I follow that ray of light to see a group of tourists dancing off-beat to the music. The bleakness of this place astounds me and makes me miss the calm of my restaurant more than ever.

Luca turns and gestures for me to go through the door.

Federico doesn't give me time to react to that foolish notion. His objection is loud and definitive. "Go," he demands, gesturing for him to walk through the door while he moves to stand between Luca and me.

Luca's face is tight with anger.

I spare a quick look at the dance floor, spotting some of my men around the perimeter. I know they know what to do if anything should happen to me.

Luca leads us down an unremarkable hallway. We pass some closed doors, and I eye them warily. Luca might have the backbone of an eel, but I would be foolish to think he isn't dangerous. Anyone can be dangerous if pushed to the brink, and he has always skirted far too close to the edge where Flavia was concerned. Unfortunately for him, he was never willing to make a big move.

"In here," Luca says.

Federico pulls his pistol from his side holster, and he gestures with the barrel for Luca to enter before me again. During this exchange, I turn in a circle, looking for another exit that doesn't go back through that same hallway, past those same closed doors. Just in case we need it. Once again, I have to content myself with the rushed nature of this meeting. We are flying by the seat of our pants. Alfonso and Giulio will be sorry they missed this.

"Padrino?"

I turn to Federico. He's inside the room, his gun and gaze still trained on Luca. "It's clear."

I nod and enter an ordinary office and check it myself. When I've confirmed Federico's assessment, I focus my gaze on Luca. He's standing nervously near a tall bookcase on the south wall. His eyes dart nervously around the room, his fingers are twitching. There's a gun. Somewhere. I know that as surely as I know that this trip is only going to get worse before it gets better.

"Wait outside," I tell Federico.

"Padrino?"

I'm sympathetic to Federico's struggle in this moment. He thinks I'm making a mistake. He knows Giulio will kill him without a second thought if anything happens to me. But I have given him a clear order.

"I'll be fine. Go."

He gives in reluctantly, stomping from the room with one more threatening glare at Luca. He closes the door behind him.

"Have a seat," I tell Luca imperiously, just to prod at him.

"This is my office," he spits.

"Do you want to piss in the corner to prove your point, or do you want to get this over with? Good," I say when he moves toward a set of four chairs around a low coffee table in the middle of the room.

"What do you want me to tell The Board?" he asks, looking cowed.

"Tell them that I am ready to retire."

I make sure that I say those words with force and not

the wistful hope I feel when I think of Shae and our baby and starting over. Of all the things I never want to share with someone like Luca, it's hope. In our line of work, that is the biggest liability of them all.

"There is no retirement, Salvatore. We both know that."

"I'm not coming to you for permission. You said you'd send my request, so send it."

He starts to reach for his pocket. My gun is in my hand before he realizes what's happened, and he freezes. "My phone," he says in a shaky voice.

"Use the one on your desk."

I keep my gun trained on him as he slowly moves across the room, his hands held carefully in the air.

"Where's Flavia?" he asks.

"Let it go. She never wanted you." I do a poor job of hiding my disgust.

"You don't know that?" He can't even say it with any surety. His voice is shaking as surely as his hands as he presses the speaker button and dials a number we both know by heart. It would have been easier if I could have made this petition on my own, but The Board loves needless formalities. Another reason I'll be happy to be rid of them.

"I do, actually. Before I killed her father, he sent her to me like a common whore. She was supposed to seduce me. Her father thought if I fucked her, I would stop trying to kill him. I wasn't interested, but she and I had a fascinating conversation about her father's allies. Including you. She told me then that you were in love with her. That her father had sent her to you the same way he sent her to me." I relish finally being able to say these words. I've been holding them in for two decades.

His face and neck are flushing a deeper shade of red. The phone rings loudly in the silence.

Finally, someone with a soft, pretty voice answers the other line with a bright, chirpy "Ciao!"

Luca gives her the message in an admirably clear voice. "I found a bird in the rafters of my bar. I need someone to come set it free."

Luca and I wait in more tense silence.

"Do you know what kind of bird it is?" she asks.

Luca shrugs. "It looks like a common pigeon. Like the ones that harass you in the Neapolitan squares. Pests." He spits that last word as an insult at me.

I smile. It's always nice to know the depths of someone else's hate matches your own.

"Okay," she says cheerily. "We will be in contact. Thank you."

Luca rudely disconnects the call without a farewell. "Tell me the rest."

"Gladly," I sneer. "She said you cried after you came and that she had to take two showers to wash your stench from her skin. No, actually, it was worse. She said you smelled like salt and sun cream, and you couldn't stay hard. And then she laughed until she cried. Her mascara was running down her face, and her lips were stained with wine. And she still tried to seduce me. She thought I would want her after that. She thought I would find her superiority seductive. Like you did. That was the problem with that family. They thought they were better than everyone else because they had money and power and could hire other people to do their dirty work. And cowards like you believe them and prop them up. You let them trifle with your life and your money while they laugh at you behind your back."

Luca looks like he's about to be sick all over his desk.

"How does it feel to know that you've wasted your life in love with a woman who thought you were Sicilian trash?"

"I don't believe you."

"You've always been a fool," I concede with a shrug.

"Where is she?"

"Dead," I say with a smile, so happy to tell someone who will care because I do not. "I killed her yesterday. I should have killed her years ago, but it was still sweet, however delayed."

Luca moves faster than I would have expected. He rips the phone from the desk and throws it at my head.

I duck out of the way, but it still clips me on the temple. The pain is sharp and stinging, but I refuse to acknowledge it because I need to survive this. Luca pulls a desk drawer open and I can only imagine what's inside, but I do not want to find out. I rush toward him and slam the butt of my gun into his face and hear the satisfying crunch of metal against skin and bone.

I would have been happy to walk out of here and let our enmity remain for whatever time we have left, but I was raised to meet force with more force.

I hear the door open and Federico's steps as he rushes

inside, but I refuse to let myself be distracted. I bring the butt of my gun down onto Luca's head again, the sounds of breaking bone, splattering blood, and gargling moans are like music to my ears.

"Padrino. Move. Let me," Federico says frantically.

"I've been waiting for this!" I scream now that I can finally let my bloodthirst loose.

Luca is bleeding beneath me, crying, moaning Flavia's name. The smell of piss is in the air.

He's pathetic to the end, and I enjoy reminding him that this is all his loyalty to her will ever get him with each hit. I slam my gun into his face until I can barely hold onto the barrel, the entire thing is slick with blood and sweat. I beat him until my back and arm are aching with the exertion.

When I'm done, when I've finally sated years of rage, I kneel next to Luca's writhing body and wipe my gun on his bloody shirt.

I stand and take a few moments to catch my breath. I feel almost as light as I did after I killed Flavia.

"She hated me," I tell Luca. I have to yell loud enough, hoping that he can hear me over his wailing. He doesn't deserve this kind of mercy, but I give it to him anyway. "She hated me for killing her father, but she hated me most for not being weak enough to let her use me. And she hated you for the exact opposite. That was the thing about Flavia; she was ruined before you ever met her."

Luca curses at me, blood and spittle seeping through his broken teeth.

I sigh and shake my head as I shoot him once in the temple and three times in the chest. The first was a kill shot. The other three are purely for my own pleasure.

I'm a simple man.

"We need to go, padrino."

I appreciate Federico's calm and the fact that he has a handkerchief on him. The performance review I give Giulio might be the best I've ever given.

I wipe at my face and follow him back into that hallway. I expect that it will be full of Luca's men, but apparently, he inspired the same kind of loyalty from them as Flavia.

What a waste of a life.

Federico and I rush through the hallway back toward the nightclub, where the volume of the music hurts my ears. At least I can rest assured that no one heard those gunshots.

Instead of pushing through the crowd on the dancefloor, Federico gestures to the rest of our men to scatter, and then he and I step through the open wall of the club directly onto the beach.

The night is cool, edging toward cold with the soft breeze from the sea. The sand gives way under my shoes. I feel the hard microscopic particles sneaking into my socks. There's a party happening further down the beach. We head for the crowd, joining the scattering of other people enjoying the night air.

I tuck my bloody gun into my holster, not worried about the mess I'm making of my clothes. In a few hours or less, everything I'm wearing will be nothing more than ash.

Federico places a quick call to arrange our pick-up. We turn at the sound of a commotion behind us. The lights in Luca's club flicker on, casting a harsh white glow on the dark sand, and the music abruptly shuts off as people rush out onto the beach, arms in front of them and their heads swiveling left and right.

So, here are Luca's men. Late. Hopefully, they learn something from this, or next time, they'll die.

At the first chance, we turn away from the water and jog up to the shore. A car pulls in front of us, and Federico pulls the back door open before the wheels stop spinning. "Come, padrino."

"If anything happens to me—"

Federico cuts me off. "It won't."

So, from all the mob movies Steve forced me to watch — a lot — and that I can remember — fewer than that — I think I'm supposed to be pretty, if not sexy. Check. A bit of a bitch. Fail. And composed while the mobster I've tied myself to goes out and does some probably...scratch that. I'm supposed to remain composed while the man I've tied myself to goes out and does some definitely heinous shit.

I'm not there yet. I'm not even remotely there yet, and I don't know that I want to reach that point.

But I manage to mostly keep myself together as Lorenzo walks me out of the club. My knees only start to shake just before I collapse into the back seat of the car. It still smells like Salvatore's cologne.

I feel like I've run a few miles in heels. I think the ridiculousness of this trip is finally taking a toll on me.

"Are you...okay?" Lorenzo asks carefully once we've pulled away from the nightclub.

"No."

"Are you hurt?" he asks in a panic.

"No. Yes."

"I don't...know what to do?" His voice is a mess of confusion, and his eyes squint at me in the rearview mirror.

"Can you go back for Salvatore?" I'm not even embarrassed by the desperation dripping from every word of that request.

"No. Are you hungry?"

"No," I bite out, but as soon as I say that, my stomach grumbles. Traitorous ass body. "I just want to go..." I almost called it home, but it's not without Salvatore there. "Just take me back to the apartment, please."

"Si, madrina," he says gently. I can hear the pity in his voice. I'm so not composed that I appreciate it. I don't care what he thinks about me; I just want Salvatore to be alright.

When we arrive back at the condo, Lorenzo pulls the car into the garage again and helps me from the back seat and into the building. This time, because I know what I'm looking for, I can see all the bodyguards stationed around the property. Some of their faces I recognize from the night we arrived, but besides Lorenzo, I don't know any of their names, so I stick closer to him than I normally would considering the fact that I don't know him either; not really.

Lorenzo says something in Italian, and the men give me some space, but not much, on Salvatore's orders, I guess. But once we make it up to the penthouse, instead of leading me past the men stationed along the hallway, Lorenzo stops at the first man.

"This is Manuele," he says. He doesn't say that I need to recognize him by sight just in case, but I can hear that warning in his voice. I look Manuele in the eye and commit as much of his face to memory as my sad, tired brain will allow.

"Nice to meet you, Manuele," I say in a quiet voice.

"Benvenuto a casa, madrina," he says slowly to make sure that I can hear and understand each word. He smiles broadly, and that sets me at ease.

We walk down the hall, stopping every few feet so that Lorenzo can introduce me to each of the men Salvatore apparently trusts to put as close to me as possible.

At the front door, Lorenzo leaves me in the hallway while he checks the entire apartment. He might be going overboard, but again, I can see why Salvatore entrusted me to him.

I wedge my body into a corner and hug myself as the fatigue starts to set in, draining me of all the energy and fear keeping me upright. It's been maybe half an hour, but it feels like forever since I left Salvatore and a little longer since Lorenzo disappeared into the apartment.

Yeah, I definitely need to eat and sleep. Maybe just sleep.

If I'm supposed to stay awake and wait for Salvatore like a good mafia wife, I'm going to have to work up to that over time and when I'm not pregnant.

"Okay," Lorenzo says, shocking me back into this dim hallway. "You can go inside."

I nod but then look up at him with the saddest expression I can muster. "Is he on the way back?"

"I don't know, but when they check in, I will tell you."

"Even if I'm asleep," I say with a yawn.

He nods and gestures toward the open door.

"Where will you—"

"Right here," he says quickly. "No one will get through me."

"'Thank you," I say quietly, reaching to close the door.

"You are good for him," he says suddenly. "He is different with you."

"Is that...a good thing? I mean...considering."

Lorenzo's smile is...terrifying, to be honest. "My uncle used to say that there is no one more dangerous than a man who suddenly has a reason to live. You are a very good thing," he says, pulling the door closed.

I'm still exhausted, but those words put a perverse smile on my face.

Okay, I have a very long way to go before I'm a good mafia movie wife, but morally compromised?

Check.

Salvatore

On the ride home, I wish I'd told Shae to stay awake for me. And I mean for me. I want to find her waiting just inside the door, naked, wet, and ready for me again because I'm a selfish asshole, and the adrenaline heating my blood hasn't dissipated yet, and it doesn't, even when I find her in the middle of the bed, my pillow clutched against her body and the covers practically covering her head.

I still want her, desperately, but not enough to disturb her. But I do think about it. My fingers even twitch at the thought of touching her, but I pull myself away, and I'm happy that I did once I see my reflection in the bathroom mirror.

There's blood matting my hairline where Luca's phone hit me. The rest of my hair is wild. My skin is sallow. And for some reason, the right side of my chest hurts.

I peel my clothes off slowly, somehow in even more pain with each lost layer. And then I see why.

"What the fuck happened to you?" Shae screams, her wide eyes trained on the bright red splotches along my right side.

"Nothing."

"Doesn't look like nothing to me. Fuck," she says, reaching for me. I flinch away from her touch. I hadn't even heard her crawl out of bed. My senses are somehow both heightened and dulled when I'm with her.

"Shae," I groan. "Bella, go back to sleep. I will be there soon."

"No," she says but turns away.

I follow her back into the room.

Instead of climbing back into bed, she pulls her suitcase from the corner of the room and turns it on its side. It's mostly empty, but she grabs a toiletry bag and turns to dump it onto the bed. She sifts through the contents until she finds the small square packet and stomps back to me.

"Take these," she says, thrusting her arm in my direction.

"I don't—"

"It wasn't a question. I'll get you some water." Once again, she rushes away from me in agitation, and once again, I follow her.

It's only as we walk toward the kitchen that I realize her nudity. The way her ass and thighs shake with each step, the tattoo at the base of her spine that I remember from the day we met, the soft rolls of just a little more flesh on each of her hips.

"Bella," I groan.

She turns to glare at me over her shoulder. Even angry, she's beautiful.

"I thought you would be happy to see me." I mean that to be a joke, but I realize that the absence of her happiness hurts even more than my ribs.

She walks right to the refrigerator and pulls a bottle of water out. I try to reach into an upper cabinet for a glass, and a pained hiss seeps from my lips.

She slaps my hand out of the way and grabs the cup instead. "I thought you were right behind me," she says, the rage still heating her words. She pours me some water and then glares at me until I do as she said and take the tablets she's given me. Only then does she relax and let me fold her carefully into my arms.

She presses her mouth to the center of my chest and then rests her cheek against my skin. "Promise me this'll be over soon."

Her voice sounds as fragile as I thought she looked the first time I saw her, but I think I know her a bit better, just enough to hear the steel underneath those words.

"I promise." It's a dangerous thing to make promises in my line of business, but I haven't lied to Shae once. So, I'll just have to make sure that anyone who might make me a liar isn't long for this world.

"Let's go bathe," I say.

She shivers against me and then finally completely relaxes. She shakes her head, and then we walk back to our bedroom together.

Not to be too Suzy fucking Homemaker, but for the next couple of days, I treat Salvatore like he's made of glass.

I cook all his meals, and we both pretend that my food is as good as his. I make sure he's comfortable at all times, shoving pillows and blankets around his side. And I watch the bruising around his ribs darken to a terrifying blue-gray. I try to convince him to go to the hospital. He might have a broken rib or three. I pretend not to be queasy when he tells me that he knows exactly what a broken rib feels like and his are just bruised. For a couple of days, I treat Salvatore with kid gloves, and to be honest, I love it.

Zoe would take my feminist card away without a second thought, but back home I know my mom's brain is tingling as if she knows that somewhere I'm cosplaying as the kind of wife she thinks all women — even Zoe — should aspire to be. It won't last, but I hope this vague awareness makes her feel good, because I don't plan to ever let her see me behaving this way.

And okay, sometimes I might treat Salvatore like a glass dildo, but in my defense, he doesn't mind at all. If I don't climb very carefully on top of him first thing in the morning, he bunches his eyebrows sadly at me and asks if something is wrong. And when I ride him slow and steady, careful where I put my hands, he massages my hips and watches me use him with the softest, most contented smile I've ever seen.

I don't know what's more shocking, that he lets me take care of him or that it makes me feel good to do so. But I do know, more and more every hour of every day, that I want exactly this life with him.

Well, not exactly this.

The only part of those two days I don't like is feeling like something is hanging over our heads. Because it is. Salvatore doesn't tell me what happened at the club after I left, and I don't ask. I decide that I don't need to know too many details; I just want whatever is happening to end.

"I want to live in the States," I say to him first thing the next morning. I'm straddling his hips, and he's just grunted and groaned while coming inside me for the first time today.

"What?" he asks, still gasping for air.

I place my hands on his chest and snake my fingers through the hair there. "When this is over, I want to move back to the States. I want to raise our baby close to my family."

His hands are caressing my thighs, but as soon as I mention the baby, one moves over my stomach, stoking my arousal even though our groins are still wet with my most recent orgasm; his tender protectiveness never ceases to turn me on.

I start to grind against him and babble without thinking. "We can, like, split our time between here and—"

"No," he says gruffly at the same time he presses his hips up into me.

I moan and move a little bit faster than I've allowed myself in days.

"We will go to America," he says. "I don't care where we live as long as we're together."

I move my hands to the bed and make sure not to grip his sides too hard with my knees, but I'm moving my hips on top of him in very determined circles, chasing another release before we've even gotten over the last one.

"You can't just leave for good."

"Bella," he whispers, wincing as he sits up, pulling me against his body.

"Be careful," I groan, wrapping my arms around his shoulders, so I can bounce on his dick.

"I don't care," he says. "You can hurt me all you want."

That sentence pulls a quick, back-bowing orgasm from me without delay. Salvatore palms my ass cheeks with both hands to keep me moving up and down the length of his shaft while I come.

"I'm almost fifty years old, bella. I've lived here for so many years without you. That's more than long enough."

I don't know what my life with Salvatore will be like in the future, but I imagine that it could just be like this. Us seeking pleasure in each other's arms while we learn how to be gentle and open with one another.

And this morning, I learn that it's possible for an orgasm to start before the previous one fully ends.

"I love you," I scream, loud enough for whoever's stationed at the door to hear.

"I love you," he whispers before taking my mouth and grunting his own release as his hips piston into mine.

"What would you like to do today?"

I'm shoving the last of some flaky, not-too-sweet pastry into my mouth. I give Salvatore my widest quizzical gaze as I chew the last of my breakfast.

He chuckles softly and takes a sip of his espresso.

"Whatever you want to do," I tell him, covering my mouth. "What *should* I do here? I never even dreamed of coming to Palermo."

He takes a contemplative sip of coffee. His eyes go soft. He scratches at his beard. "I don't know." Those three words seem to distress him. I think this is the first time I've ever seen him look at an actual loss for words, and it endears him to me. I wonder if this is what our child will look like, all pursed mouth and bunched bushy eyebrows.

God, I hope so.

"How do you have a house here, but you don't know

any tourist attractions at least?" I ask the question playfully, but the look on his face makes my heart break, like shatter into a million pieces, dust.

"I don't come here often. Actually, this is the longest I've ever been here."

"Why?" I gasp at the same time I begin to reach for the half-eaten pastry on his plate.

He wasn't going to finish it anyway. Probably.

Anyway, it's gone before he even has an answer to my question.

"Years ago, this apartment was my dream."

"That's not a bad dream."

He smiles sadly and takes another sip of his coffee. "It was also a good investment."

I nod like I know what the fuck that's like. I'm *broke*-broke, and I own even less than I did when he and I met.

"Although in the end, it was just one more thing I bought that I never really had the opportunity to enjoy."

"But why? Aren't you the boss? Isn't that the point of being the head of like...whatever it is you're doing?"

I know he's much older than me, but I see the years between us in a new way right now. His eyes are rimmed red with exhaustion, and our age gap feels at least twice as big as it really is.

"I chose this, bella," he says gravely. "This is who I am. When I started traveling down this path, I knew getting to the top of the ladder wouldn't be easy, but I did imagine it would be the end. I thought it would give me the kind of freedom I always craved."

"But it didn't."

He shakes his head, slow and sad. "Every step only gave me more responsibilities. Every day I woke up with more people looking to me for orders and answers and protection."

"And more enemies?"

He takes another sip of coffee with a smile. "I've never minded the enemies, actually. That was the easy part."

"Easy?" My voice breaks, and I can feel the pressure of tears like a familiar companion.

Have I ever cried this much in my entire adult life? No.

Salvatore reaches for me, and I close my eyes at the feeling of his hands on me again. The constant pleasure of just having him touch me is intoxicating. My body starts to turn to jelly, and soon enough, my panties will be clinging to my wet lips again, just from his strong hand caressing the back of my neck.

"If you weren't here, this would be easier. Survival has always been much less interesting to me than power."

Those words remind me of Salvatore's father and his lessons, but, try as I might, I can't see the danger in Salvatore's eyes. I know he *is* dangerous, but I also know that he'd never hurt me. And it might be foolish and naïve, but in this moment, I realize that this is all that matters. Not hurting me and our children is all I'll ever ask of him.

"I want to go to the beach," I tell him.

"Whatever you want." His smile is feral and elegant; so eager.

I scoot my chair back from the table and lower myself

to my knees. "But not right now," I tell him, crawling between his legs and reaching for the button of his pants.

"Whatever you want, bella," he replies in a heated whisper, brushing his fingers across the tops of my cheeks.

And then groaning loudly as I take him into my mouth.

"I DIDN'T THINK THIS THROUGH," Shae says, frowning adorably at the sea. The weather is mild, but the blue water is darker than normal, not at all like the beautiful, light, clear blue in some of the posters we saw while on our short walk from the apartment.

"It is the off-season," I concede. "But it is still beautiful." I try to offer her some hope.

She looks skeptically around us at the mostly empty beach with a frown on her face. "Is it?" she asks in a wispy, disbelieving voice.

"Si, bella." I let go of her hand and wrap my arm around her shoulders, pulling her into my side. I love the way she melts against me each time as if it's new.

"Are you sure this is okay?" she whispers. "Are you sure we're safe?" Her breath tickles the edges of my beard.

"You're always safe with me. Do you want to take our shoes off and walk in the sand?"

"No. I hate sand, actually."

I stop walking and turn toward her in confusion. "Then why did you want to come to the beach?"

She shrugs in my arms. "I don't know. You seemed like you wanted to do something besides stay in the apartment and fuck. This was all I could come up with."

"I...didn't want that. I thought you would want that."

Now the disbelief is in her face as well as her voice. "What the fuck would make you think that? I like food. I like art. I like sleep. And to be honest, with all that's been going on in my life, we can swap art out for sex. Food, sex, sleep sounds like the best day."

"Bella, why didn't you say anything?" I ask, trying to keep my voice even.

"Why didn't you ask me?" She smiles impishly up at me, wrapping both arms around my waist. "I guess we'll have to learn how to communicate better?"

"I've never—"

"Yeah, me neither," she says, brushing her mouth over mine.

"Do you want to go back?"

She shakes her head and steps away. Well, she tries to, but I refuse to let her get away from me so easily ever again. "I've worked up an appetite now. That was such a long walk."

"It was ten minutes, maybe less. We can still see the building from here."

"I'm pregnant. It was so long," she says, smiling. "I bet this city has the best seafood restaurants."

She looks so hopeful and excited; how can I tell her

that I'm not hungry, or that the restaurants, like the beaches, are off-season as well?

"Let us discover this together, no?"

She shrugs and looks over my shoulder. "Us and our friends." She waves at my men, and then her face lights up. "Manuele."

"What?"

"I don't remember him from the plane."

"No..." I say in slow confusion.

"So, he's from here, right?"

"Ah, yes. Yes." I call Lorenzo to us. We walk along the shore while someone locates Manuele to tell us where to eat because Shae wants seafood, and I'll make sure she gets it.

———

We send Manuele to the restaurant to arrange our lunch. By the time we arrive, Shae is becoming grumpier by the moment, and I find that adorable. Almost adorable enough to slow my steps on the way to the restaurant, but she threatens me fiercely.

Adorable and harmless, but I still comply. Anything to make her happy.

She leans into my side as we walk up to a reserved rooftop dining area. All along the perimeter of the structure are hanging plants. The muted green is calming, but I imagine in the spring and summer, this place would be bursting full of life and colors. Like the beach, it would have been nice to see it in summer, but with Shae here, there's more than enough sunshine.

"Seriously?" she gasps with a wide smile and bright eyes.

I press a kiss to the side of her head, inhaling the scent of whatever she used on her hair. Inhaling her.

"How did you even—?"

"I have rarely gotten to appreciate all this power that I've been accumulating over the years."

She nods, confused.

"But now, I can spoil you, so none of it has to go to waste."

"I—" She shakes her head, and I cannot help but marvel at her innocence.

I've spent years wielding my power in ways that solidified my position, but nothing ever made me this happy. Every moment with her is joyful.

"It's so beautiful."

I pull her into my arms and press my mouth to her ear. "Nothing will ever be more beautiful than you."

"I want to make memories with you."

It's my turn to be speechless. I thought hearing her gasp that she loves me into my ear was all I needed.

"This is the kind of stuff I want to tell our baby about in the future. Days like this."

"You mean you don't want to tell our child how we met?"

Her smile is breathtaking. "Of course. But I've already started editing it in my head."

"Oh?" I lead her toward a table in the center of the room.

"Not a lot," she says. "But I think we can leave out everything after the pizza."

I pull her chair out, and she sits. I kiss her behind her right ear.

"Bella?" I say, licking her earlobe.

She moans and turns her head just a little bit to get closer to my mouth.

"I promise you'll have to edit today as well."

It pains me that this is the first promise to Shae I cannot keep.

But I'll make sure it's the last.

Shae

Salvatore orders almost half the menu while I giggle, and my stomach growls louder by the second.

Our waiter is red-faced and shaking like a leaf, trying to balance writing down the dishes Salvatore wants me to try and glancing nervously at all of the bodyguards around the dining area.

My only contribution to this process is to whisper very loudly, "Make sure you get some bread."

He smiles and finishes the order.

"Vino?" the waiter asks.

"No," we say quickly.

"Just water, please."

"Acqua frizzante," he says, dismissing the boy with a warm smile.

He doesn't run away, but I can tell that he wants to.

I'm certain that I should feel some way about that — that I'm with a man who makes people want to run — but when I look at Salvatore again, I can't fathom it. I can't imagine not wanting to spend all my time with him. The longer we're together — the more he makes me come — I can't even picture a future with anyone else.

I think it's the way he looks at me. No, it *is* the way he looks at me.

He sits back in his chair, crosses his legs, and rests his chin in his hand. He looks so much like he did the day we met, except now I know what he feels like inside me and what his come tastes like on my tongue. I'm not wondering and ruining that mental exploration with an echoing guilt because 'what about Steve?' There's no Steve, only Salvatore, and that thought makes me smile.

"Are you happy?" he asks, his voice going low, his accent thickening.

"Yes," I reply breathlessly. "Are you happy?"

"Like never before, but you know what would make me happier?"

Dear Jesus, I've never nodded faster or felt so eager in my life.

But I have been this horny since the moment Salvatore and I were alone in that apartment in Naples. Hell, since the first day I met him. Even when we were apart, I think I was just a banked fire, waiting for him to reignite the flame inside me.

I wonder what he's going to tell me. What he's going to tell me to do. What I want him to tell me to do, but he's determined to make me wait.

Salvatore

"Do they not bring bread in Italy? Is that not a thing here?" she asks, kicking my foot under the table playfully; impatiently. "Or water? Didn't we order water?"

"We did." I glance at Federico, and he dashes down the stairs to the main floor of the restaurant.

"What should we do after this?"

I lift my eyebrows. "Home," I say. "We have plans."

Her foot slides along mine up to my ankle. "Do we?" she asks, a slow smile spreading across her face.

"Shae."

"I'm hungry. I forgot. You should remind me."

I'm out of my chair in a heartbeat. We do have plans, and all I can think about is the fastest way to make her come now. I don't care who's around to see it.

But the moment is interrupted by shouting from the bottom of the stairs.

We all turn at the sound, but I don't stop. I learned that early — a moving target is harder to hit. I circle around the table and pull Shae as gently as I can from her chair. "Come, bella."

"What's—" she starts to ask and then stops, rushing from her chair and grabbing my hand.

My god, I couldn't love her more.

There's a door behind the stairs that leads to another stairwell. I'd spotted it on the way in because it's natural for me to be aware of my surroundings. Shae and I sprint toward the door behind Lorenzo while the rest of my men split between covering our exit and rushing down the other stairs to help Federico.

"Come, padrino," Lorenzo says. He pulls his gun from his holster. "I will go first."

I nod and let go of Shae's hand to pull my own gun from the holster under my arm.

"Wait, have you had that on you the entire time?"

"Not now, my love." I send her out onto the metal stairs after Lorenzo so I can watch our backs.

After the commotion from the restaurant, the world outside seems peaceful. Sure, I can hear people hawking their delicacies at a nearby market, but there's no gunfire, and besides our shoes clanging on the steps, it's peaceful.

Relatively.

Lorenzo makes it off the steps first, and he lifts his gun, heading toward the mouth of the alley quickly but cautiously.

Shae steps into the alley and immediately turns to look up at me. She's shaking and throws her arms over her stomach protectively. Seeing that makes my heart pound against my chest.

The silence breaks in an instant.

The door above us slams open. I hear someone shouting, but I can't make out exactly what they're saying. I'm only focused on getting to Shae, and I grab her hand in mine before I take the final step from the metal stairs. She squeezes my one hand with both of hers.

We turn toward the mouth of the alley just in time to hear Lorenzo yell and a burst of gunshots.

Shae gasps and screams. Lorenzo falls to the ground.

I pull Shae behind me and lift my gun level with my chest to set my sights on Pedro Lombardi.

"Hello, Salvo."

"What are you doing here?"

"You called us."

"That was two days ago. You know where I live and how to reach me."

Pedro has the nerve to shrug and smile as if I'm not aiming a gun directly at his head. But his men have more than one aimed at me, so he probably assumes that he's safe.

As if he can read my thoughts, Pedro leans to the side, smiling at Shae. "Ciao, bella. Benvenuti a Sicilia."

Shae's hands are pressed against my shoulder blades, and I feel her move behind me, shrinking away from Pedro's gaze. But it doesn't matter; Pedro has made his point. I will give him that.

"Don't talk to her. Look at me," I grind out, my grip tightening on the gun.

It would take very little effort to kill him. One shot right between the eyes. He's close enough that I could do it with my eyes closed. If I were alone, I would have, for the disrespect alone.

Lorenzo groans weakly. I don't look away from Pedro,

but I can hear by the whimpering cry behind me and a gasp that Shae does.

"You could have called me in," I spit out. "That *is* why I'm here."

Pedro crosses his arms in front of him and shrugs again. "Under other circumstances, that might have been an option, but these are not normal times."

I grind my teeth together.

"The Board has heard some distressing rumors."

"Has The Board turned into a gaggle of gossiping old women recently?"

Pedro laughs, airy and fake. "There are also...accusations that you need to account for."

"Watch your mouth." Pedro might have a lot of men, he might even have the upper hand in this moment, but he is nothing more than an errand boy. He might have forgotten that, but I have not.

"Mi scuso, padrino. The Board requests your attendance to answer some pressing questions."

"Fine," I say. "I'll be happy to come."

Shae's fingers dig into my shirt. "No," she says, so low I only hear because she's practically molded her body against my back.

"Let me just calm her down."

"No," Pedro says quickly. "I've been told to bring your woman with you."

"She's not a part of this."

"Of course, she's not, but only a fool would try and bring you in without...a contingency plan." He punctuates the dramatic pause with a sharp, menacing smile.

Pedro has always delighted in his role as henchman, more than even Alfonso. However, I know that threat isn't for me; it's for Shae.

She's shaking against me, and if I do nothing else, I'll make sure that Pedro pays for this.

"You shot my man," I say, stalling for time.

"I apologize for that. We'll happily get him and your other injured men some assistance as soon as we leave."

"Padrino, no," Lorenzo groans from the ground.

"The loyalty you inspire really is legendary," Pedro says smugly. "You don't want that to be in vain, do you?"

This was not the plan, thin as it was. The only thing that mattered was keeping Shae as far away from this as possible, and the rage I feel that I couldn't do even that makes my index finger twitch. Pedro is still in my sights.

It would be so easy. It would be worth the consequences to myself.

But if Shae was harmed, that wouldn't be worth whatever momentary release I would get.

I lower my hand and set the lock on my gun. One of Pedro's men rushes forward to grab the gun from me. I turn and grab Shae's hands. She's shaking like a delicate leaf. Her eyes are rimmed red, and her cheeks are wet.

"I am so sorry, bella. You have to come with me."

Her fingers tangle with mine, and she nods her head quickly. "Okay." That one word breaks my heart.

Pedro says something that I ignore.

"Will he be okay?" she asks, glancing quickly down at Lorenzo.

"Of course, he will," Pedro yells. "If we leave soon."

I begin to pull Shae toward the car along the curb. As we pass, I look at Lorenzo, struggling on the ground, and fix him in my gaze. "Relax," I tell him. "Don't bleed out. I still need you."

"Padrino." He winces as he says that word.

Shae turns to look at Lorenzo, and I have to pull her along with gentle promises that he will recover.

Promises that make Pedro chuckle.

I add his laughter to the list of reasons The Board will regret taking me in this way.

I HOPE that when we arrive in Palermo, everything will be explained. I call Salvatore as soon as we land, and his mobile phone is turned off. It doesn't even ring anymore. Maybe it's dead.

Maybe he's dead.

I call Federico while we wait for the plane door to open, but his phone just rings and rings.

I try Lorenzo next; switching back and forth between them like I have since last night.

When I hear Lorenzo's weak voice on the other end of the line, I stop walking immediately, and my heart starts racing.

"Giulio," the other man says.

"Where the fuck have you been? Where is Salvo?"

He takes a slow, labored breath while I fight the urge to scream.

"What's going on?" Alfonso says. "Where are they?"

He's huddling close to me, trying to hear, but I can't put the call on speakerphone.

"Where are you, Giulio?"

"Where are you?" I say, much louder and with more force than I mean.

"At the hospital. Are you at the airport?"

"Yes. What hospital?"

"It doesn't matter. Tommaso will collect you, and we'll talk when you arrive." He hangs up, and I don't scream necessarily, but a woman does clutch her children to her side at my loud grunt. I scowl at her.

"What hospital?" Alfonso asks.

"Yeah, what fucking hospital?"

The sound of Zahra's voice makes my heart stop pounding for a brief moment. Alfonso and I turn to see Zahra and Zoe staring at us, fear and anger warring on their faces, their arms crossed over their chests.

"If you don't tell us what the fuck is going on right now, I promise you'll regret it for the rest of your life," Zahra says.

"If not longer." Alfonso tenses at Zoe's addition.

"I—"

"Giulio! Alfonso! Benvenuti!"

We all turn to see Tommaso walking toward us with a wide smile and his arms thrown open. He's making a scene on purpose. I wish I could tell him that he doesn't have to bother; we've taken care of that already. I also want to know whose attention he's trying to attract.

I need to know what's going on now.

Tommaso chatters incoherently as he makes his way

to us. He hustles Alfonso into a hug, but when he reaches for me, I glare at him, and he stops.

"Come on, Giulio," he says, "put on a show." Normally I would say no, but I notice that his eyes and his smile seem strained.

I let him pull me into what I hope will be a quick hug, but Tommaso holds on tight.

"He told us not to answer your calls."

"Why the fuck would he do that?"

"Just in case someone was listening in. But he knew you would come after a while."

I curse Salvo in a way I never would to his face. If he hears about this and punishes me, at least he will be alive. "Where is he, Tommaso?"

"With The Board," he whispers.

I try to pull away, but he has a sure grip on me.

"Just come with me, and I'll tell you everything, but not here."

I nod, and he finally lets me go. Every tendon in my body is pulled taut, and it's taking me much more effort than it should to remain in control.

Tommaso holds my face with both hands. "Smile, Giulio. Everything will be fine as long as we follow the plan."

"What. Fucking. Plan?" Zahra and Zoe grind those three words out as if all the tendons in their bodies are pulled taut as well.

Tommaso turns around and smiles. "Salve signore," he says, throwing his arms wide. "Beauti—"

"Not interested, string bean," Zoe says dismissively.

"Get out of the way. We're busy threatening them. The fuck?" Zahra adds.

Tommaso deflates between us and looks over his shoulder at Alfonso. "Are they...with you?"

"Very," Alfonso replies. "And I would do what they say."

"I—"

"You heard him," Zahra says in a threatening tone.

"Amore, please," I say, stepping around Tommaso.

"Please, my ass," she hisses.

Alfonso snickers. "Grow up," Zoe says, even though she's laughing as well.

"Tell me," Zahra says, backing away from me.

I reach for her and pull her into my arms. She clutches my shirt in her delicate fists. I wish I could kiss away the stress from her face. "I don't know what's happening."

"But something *is* happening?"

I nod and brush my mouth over the tops of her cheeks. "I'll fix it," I promise.

"You can't—"

"Yes, I can." I nudge her nose with mine until she lifts her head and puckers her lips for me.

I brush my mouth across hers. "If anything happens to my cousin—"

"As long as she's with Salvo, I think she'll be safe."

"How do you know?"

"Because he looked at her the same way I look at you."

"Which is how?" she whispers, her tongue darting out to tease my lips.

"He looks at Shae as if the only thing that will stop him from protecting her is a bullet to the head." I take her lips, quick and hard. I taste the depths of her mouth, reminding her that we can weather this storm; we can survive anything together.

When I pull away, Zahra has a dreamy smile on her face. "When this is over," she whispers. "Then you can please my ass. But not a second before."

I imagine that the next few hours, maybe days will be dangerous, but Zahra always knows how to give me something to look forward to.

"Can we chill with all the PDA in the airport?" Zoe says.

"Oh, you don't like that?" Alfonso says. "Since when?"

Zahra pulls away from me. "Check fucking mate!" she calls excitedly. "I love him for you."

Zoe rolls her eyes. "Can we get out of here?"

"Yes, please. Follow me," Tommaso says, leading the way like an excited tour guide.

It's only because I know him so well that I notice the way his head keeps scanning in every direction, checking to make sure that we're not being followed. Or maybe that we are.

When we arrive at Salvatore's condominium building, Alfonso takes the girls to an empty apartment, and Tommaso takes me up to the penthouse.

"Tell me," I say as soon as I step into the condo. Tommaso catches me up while I search the apartment.

"They weren't taken from here."

I nod, but I keep searching. Salvo would expect me not to skip a single step.

"When Salvo arrived, I took him to see..."

"Flavia," I finish for him. "What happened?"

"He talked with her for a while. I don't know about what," he adds before I can ask. "But whatever she told him was useful."

"Did he kill her?"

"Yes."

"Good. What happened next?"

"Lorenzo and Federico will tell you the details. All I know is that he wanted an audience with The Board, and he went to Luca Giordano to make the request."

I stop at that name. I've checked the living room, dining area, and kitchen. I haven't found anything out of order. But that name surely is. There are few people Salvatore hates; Luca is one. "And what happened?"

"According to my contact at the coroner's office, they found Luca's body yesterday."

"Yesterday?"

Tommaso shrugs. "Apparently, Luca's men didn't notice he was missing for a while."

I grunt. "I wonder if there was any money left in his

accounts. I'm sure The Board will want to hear about that."

"I assume so."

"Were you not there?"

Tommaso shakes his head. "Salvo gave me another job."

"Which was?"

"I think I should tell you and Alfonso that together."

I squint my eyes and frown. "Why?"

Tommaso smiles, big and bright. "Because that was part of the job. Salvo told me whenever you got here, it would be time to start the final stage of his plan."

"Whenever I got here?" I yell. "If he wanted us here, why didn't he just call us?"

Tommaso holds up his hands and shrugs. "You might question the boss, but I don't. Anyway, I'm gonna go downstairs. Take your time. We have time."

"How do you know that?"

He rolls his eyes. "I told you, Salvo has a plan."

At that, Tommaso walks to the front door and pulls it open, waving on his way out.

I'm so angry that I glare at the closed door for a few minutes after he's gone, trying to calm my racing pulse. When I have myself together, I walk down the hall to check the bedrooms. The guest room is mostly empty and pristine, a bed that no one has slept in taking up most of the space. The master bedroom makes my gut clench. Shae's presence is everywhere; her bonnet on her pillow, her pajamas thrown over the foot of the bed, her toothbrush next to Salvo's on the bathroom sink.

I have to find Salvo. That's my job. He's my boss and friend. I owe him this. But I also *have* to find Shae. I don't know how I can look Zahra in the eyes again if I don't. I don't know how she'll be able to stay with me if I fail.

I walk to the last bedroom. It's Salvo's office. Even I've never been in here. I reach for the door handle, expecting it to be locked. When I find that it's open, my gut clenches.

Salvo's offices are a window into his brain and I find exactly what I expect. The room is tidy with a small couch under the window on one side of the room, a large armoire taking up the opposite wall, a rug in the middle of the room, and a desk across from the door with boxes neatly stacked on it. I can see two small slips of paper on top of the pile of boxes. I walk to the desk, hoping that I'll find answers here, and I guess I do.

One of the envelopes is addressed to Shae. The only thing that stops me from opening it is knowing that Salvo will kill me if he finds out that I have. And he will find out because he *will* be back.

Besides, the other envelope is addressed to me. "Why didn't you just call me?" I mutter, ripping it open.

"Ai, cazzo," I groan as I read his words. "Why is nothing ever easy with you?" I say as if Salvo is in the room. But he's not. And whatever Tommaso thinks, I don't talk back to the boss either. But when I get Salvo out of this, I will give him a piece of my mind for taking such unnecessary risks.

A piece.

A small piece.

Alfonso

"What's going on?" Zoe hisses against my ear.

"How would I know?" I ask with a laugh, which is a mistake.

She jabs her fist into my side, and I groan.

"Why are you laughing? My cousin is missing."

"She's not missing," Federico calls from across the room. He's standing behind a brooding Lorenzo, who is sitting in a chair with a murderous scowl on his face.

"We know where she is," Lorenzo says. The man looks to be trying to burn a hole into the floor with his eyes.

"We'll get her back," Federico says, placing a hand carefully on Lorenzo's shoulder, but the other man still flinches at his touch.

"I like him," Zoe says. "He understands the stakes."

I squint at her. "We need to get Salvo back."

She shrugs. "Yeah, him too, I guess."

"Zoe," Zahra calls from the couch, a soft warning in the way she says her sister's name.

"I said, *I guess.* I met the man once. What more do you want from me?"

I press my mouth against her temple.

Giulio rushes into the room and heads straight to Zahra. Zoe and I watch her wrap her arms around his shoulders and whisper to him. The scowl on Giulio's face doesn't disappear, but it does soften.

I lean into Zoe's side. "Will that be us in a few months?"

She scowls at me. "I'll leave you before we're ever that cheesy."

"I can hear you," Zahra says.

"Good, girl, our cousin is missing. You can stop cupcakin' for a hot second so we can find her, can't you?"

"We'll find her," Lorenzo says.

"We'll find them both," Giulio echoes.

"Great, now that we're on the same page," Tommaso says. "Let's get down to business, shall we?"

"Please," Zoe says.

We all turn to Tommaso, and he walks to the front door. I stop smiling and move in front of Zoe. Out of the corner of my eye, I see the other men reach for their guns, but I freeze when I see who walks through the door.

"Capo," Giulio says, standing quickly.

"What's going on?" I aim at Tommaso.

The man smiles. "I told you, Salvatore gave me a job to do." He gestures toward the other man. "He wanted to make sure that I brought you all together."

"Why?" Giulio, Lorenzo, Federico, and I all ask at the same time.

"Because he had a proposition for you, capo, and orders for you," he says, turning to the rest of us.

The room is silent as we take this in. I usually try not to do this, but for the first time in a long time, I try to figure out what exactly Salvatore has up his sleeves.

"Okay, you know what? I think I could like Sal after

all. 'Cause whatever is going on is some mastermind-level shit," Zoe says.

"I told you he was elegant," Zahra says.

Tommaso laughs loudly. "An elegant mastermind. I think Salvatore would like that label."

"If he lives," the capo says in a sober, crisp voice, reminding us of the actual stakes.

He takes a seat in a hard-backed chair in the middle of the room. We all sit after him — the men. Zoe and Zahra never bothered to stand.

The capo crosses his legs. "What is Salvatore's proposition? I respect him enough to hear him out, but I will not promise more than that."

My eyes dart to Giulio. It's a death sentence to kill a capo, but in a split second of eye contact, I know that we are both ready to take that chance.

We respect Salvatore enough to try.

Zahra

I don't understand any of what's going on and not just because the men are moving between English and Italian without a care for the monolingual among us. I can't help but wonder if Zoe and I should even be here, but each time that question surfaces, I yank it back.

Shae is our baby cousin. Of course, we should be here, even if I have no fucking idea how we can help.

I should also be here because I want to be by Giulio's

side. But to do that, I *definitely* need to learn Italian fast because there will only be more meetings going right over my head, and how can I be helpful to him like that?

Although, actually, language barrier notwithstanding, I'm smart, and it's not *all* escaping me. I'm clever enough to pick up on a few key things.

First, whoever the hell this man is, he's powerful as fuck. So powerful that he strolled in here without a bodyguard and, judging from the easy look on his face, without a care in the world that any of Sal's men will betray him. Based on what I've observed in my short few weeks with Giulio and all the mob movies I love, there's only one thing that could make someone this bold. *Power.* A fucking grip of it. Maybe even more of it than Sal.

To be honest, that makes me shudder. Giulio squeezes my knee reassuringly, but he doesn't take his eyes off of the man sitting in the center of the room. And I guess that's another indication that this man is the real deal.

Secondly, this is a takeover — I think. I'm sure I miss a lot of the intricacies and most of the history, but I also think that if Sal's proposition was presented in a boardroom, this would all seem very normal. I'm not trying to rehabilitate the mob or anything, but from what I've heard from my corporate friends, this kind of treachery is very normal, just without guns.

But what really gets me is all the holes in this plan.

"You cannot be serious?" I didn't mean to blurt that out, but...it had to be said. Didn't it? Okay, maybe it didn't because the way almost every man in the room turns to glare at me is a bit intense. Even Giulio is looking at me like I've lost my mind.

"Smooth," Zoe snickers.

I'll get her back for that later.

"What happens if they're like…having that trial now?" I aim that question at Giulio because he looks leagues nicer than every other man in the room right now.

"They will not have the trial without me," the man says. "And who are you?"

"Um, I—" I am terrified at this man looking at me. I don't think I want him to even know I exist now that he does. Lord, I wish I could rewind time.

"We're Shae's cousins," Zoe answers in my stead.

I let out a shaky breath, happy for the reminder that I'm not the only outsider here.

Giulio squeezes my knee again. "And Zahra will be my wife."

"Excuse me?" Zoe squeals.

I blink at Giulio.

"Hello, I said, *excuse me?*" Zoe says again.

"What exactly has been going on in Naples?" the other man asks, his voice thawing just a little bit. He sounds…interested in a way that I do not like because I don't want anyone that powerful interested in me. Except Giulio. But he's not on that rung of the power ladder yet, by far.

I turn to my sister, and she and I have twin "aw, shit" looks on our faces. Maybe we can't save Shae until we save ourselves.

But Giulio squeezes my knee again. "With all respect, that's none of your business," he says.

Zoe mouths, "Oh my God," to me.

I frown in her direction. "It was nice knowing you," I whisper.

Giulio keeps squeezing my knee in rhythmic, reassuring presses of his hand. "We're here to relay Salvo's offer, not explain the developments in his territory to you."

"Is it still his territory?" the man asks. Everyone in the room visibly stiffens, and the quiet that descends on us feels deadly.

Giulio loves his guns, and he has reached for them for far less disrespect to Sal. So I can only guess that the reason he hasn't pulled the pistol from the holster under his arm is out of respect for whoever this man is. Or fear. It could definitely also be fear.

"Yes," Giulio grinds out through a clenched jaw, speaking for the other men in the room.

I watch as the man's eyes scan the room. He skips over Zoe and I — which is rude, but I'm not going to complain. I've learned my lesson. But I do watch as he takes stock of Sal's men silently, slowly, before coming to some decision.

He shakes out his hand and looks at the watch on his wrist. "I will let Salvatore know my answer at the meeting."

"But—" Zoe starts. Alfonso quiets her before she can make the same mistake I did.

Still, that one word was enough to grab his attention,

and he looks at Zoe and I with the same kind of focus he gave the men. I don't like it. He comes to another decision, and just like the first, he doesn't bother to share.

"I have to go," he says, standing abruptly. "I have other business to attend to."

Once again, all the men stand, and Tommaso steps forward to usher him out.

"Wait," Giulio says.

"Babe, shh," I whisper.

The man looks at me briefly, and I think he *almost* smiles, but like a really far-off almost.

Giulio walks past him to the front door. There's a black gift box on the table by the door. He opens it and shows the man what's inside. I crane my neck, but it's hard to see from the couch.

"Is that...?" the man starts, moving his hand to touch it but stopping. Staring.

"Yes. Salvo told me to tell you that if you agree to the deal, then you know what to do with this."

Up until now, the man has been calm, cool, and collected, but whatever's in that box has affected him enough that he stands there, staring at it, his hand still poised to touch it but frozen. It's as if he takes all the air out of the room, and we sit or stand in silence, hanging on a small ledge, waiting to see what he will do next.

Because so much relies on this one man, apparently.

"I will consider it," he says in a rough voice. He takes the box from Giulio's hand carefully, staring down at its contents for a few seconds more before closing the lid slowly. And with that, he sweeps out of the room with Tommaso on his heels.

"Yo, what the fuck was all that?" Zoe breathes.

"Is it too early for a glass of wine?" I ask nervously.

"Everything will be okay," Giulio says. I want to believe him, and so I decide that I will, just like I've decided to stay right here by his side.

Lord, I hope I know what I'm getting myself into.

I KNOW I'm dreaming immediately because when Salvatore smiles at me, the fear in my stomach doesn't disappear in a wave of naïve affection and lust. It gets worse, and that's never happened before. For better or worse, from the moment I met Salvatore, he's always been able to chase away my anxieties and most of my common sense.

I wake up with a start, but I don't move — can't move.

"I'm here, bella," Salvatore whispers against my forehead, hugging me close to his chest.

I rub my face against his shirt and wrap myself around his torso. In the back of my mind, I'm thinking that if I can just rub him the right way, this can all be over, except I have no idea what all this even is.

In the American movies, when the mobster gets kidnapped, sometime later, the cops find his body in a river or something. It can't be that different in Italy, can it?

Apparently, it can.

We climbed into the back seat of that mobster's car yesterday, and I thought that was it. Lorenzo's pained groans were ringing in my ears, and I just knew that soon enough, Salvatore's would join them before the day was over. I sat in the back seat, shuddering so hard my teeth were clacking together. The only thing that stopped me from screaming was Salvatore's arms around me and Pedro's constant yammering about Palermo like he was on the damn tourism board. Instead of like, I don't know, throwing a bag over my head, he spent the entire ride pointing through the front window at local landmarks he didn't want me to miss. It was weird and only got weirder when we arrived at our destination. Which wasn't, by the way, like a prison or whatever, but a large villa with the most breathtaking view of the sea.

We're in the middle of nowhere, and if we tried to run away, we'd probably get nowhere fast, so maybe that's why Pedro seemed completely at ease, but I don't know if that explains why he gave us a tour of the villa like it was a luxury hotel. I mean, it looks like one, but still.

I'd been numb with shock, but Salvatore behaved as if this was all very normal. As if there was nothing odd in what was happening at all. He even made sure to inquire about dinner since we'd never gotten to eat all the food we'd ordered. Dinner arrived. Salvatore tasted everything to make sure it was safe, and then he'd fed me, showered with me, and held me while I cried myself to sleep because the stress was too much.

And that was how I spent my first night as a prisoner. I've never had cause to wonder what being kidnapped would be like, but all the movies I've seen lied to me.

"We're still here," I groan, still rubbing my cheek against Salvatore's chest.

"We are. Hopefully, it will not be for much longer."

I sit up in bed a little too fast, and I feel queasy. I close my eyes, and Salvatore sits up next to me, rubbing my arms. "Bella?"

I shake my head quickly and then regret that. "It's just morning sickness," I say. "Or stress. Both?"

He presses his mouth against my temple.

"Did something happen while I was asleep?"

Salvatore pulls back.

"Why won't we be here much longer? Did I miss something?"

I won't pretend that I've ever felt as if Salvatore was an open book, but I have generally thought that I could ask him whatever I wanted and get an answer — some answer — until right now.

Salvatore keeps rubbing my arms and back, looking at me with those clear, penetrating eyes and what looks like a smile dying to break out on his lips.

Very weird.

"What's going on? What—"

He shakes his head slowly, not telling me no, I realize, simply asking that I not ask him a question he cannot answer. Yet.

"When this is over?" I whisper.

"I will tell you everything. I will give you everything."

"I'm going to hold you to that," I tell him as fiercely as I can before I break into a loud yawn.

"Come, my love."

Salvatore crawls out of bed. He's wearing a long-sleeved button-down shirt and pants pajama set that matches mine. Since we didn't have any clothes with us, I think it's very nice that our hotel-prison provided the basics. I would have also liked a scarf for my hair since that Bantu knot twist out was already struggling, but I survived a night on cotton pillowcases. Although, if we get out of here and there's an online survey, I have some suggestions.

But until then, I watch as Salvatore wears the hell out of the old-school pajama set, looking elegant and also somehow sexy. This might be the hormones talking. Or the stress.

Either way. "Where are we going?" I ask, pushing the covers from my body. I only wore the shirt, and the cool air in the room gives me goosebumps across my bare legs.

"The bathroom. You will feel better after a bath."

This is not a dream because when Salvatore saunters around the bed, watching me, the heavy length of his dick swaying as he walks, confusion and fear give way to desire.

"Okay!" I practically scream, scrambling to my feet.

I'll make room for fear later.

"Really?" I whine.

"Really," Salvatore says easily as he moves the wash-cloth over every inch of my back. From outside of the bathtub.

"I thought we were going to take a bath together." I'm pouting like a child — or trying to; the scrubbing and hot water feel amazing.

"Believe that I want nothing more than that, but today will be a busy day."

I don't know what that means, and right now, I don't want to. I bend my legs and wrap my arms around my shins. I turn my head, resting my cheek on my knees so I can look at him. "That's even more reason to take a bath with me. You can relax before...whatever's coming comes."

Salvatore brushes an index finger along my hairline. "Tempting."

"Good. That was the point."

He laughs. "But I need to stay focused. Sit back."

I grunt and do what he says, leaning against the high end of the soaker tub. "Seriously, is this like a hotel? Where the fuck are we?"

He dips the washcloth back into the water and then begins to scrub my neck. "This house is owned by..." He stops talking and squints here as if he's searching for the right word or translating a word from Italian that maybe has no English equivalent. "My associates," he settles on ominously.

"Nice save," I mutter.

He moves the cloth over my left breast, stimulating

my nipple, and I groan. He smiles triumphantly before he continues.

"They use this villa for official business."

"And you're official business?"

"I've petitioned to leave the organization."

I gasp just as Salvatore's hand begins to circle the swell of my stomach. He looks at me seriously again, and I keep the many questions sprouting in my mind to myself. Only one of them matters, though. I want to ask if he's leaving for me, but don't I already have that answer since I'm here? So, I ask what I think is the safest question. "Can you...do that? Leave, I mean?"

His hand dips below the waterline to clean my hips and thighs. "It isn't unheard of, but it is rare."

"But it could happen?" I am so goddamn eager that even I'm embarrassed, but I need to hold onto any shred of hope I can. Because I get it — this might not be the kidnapping I expected, but this is still captivity.

Salvatore tries to let me down gently. "I don't know, bella. I can only make the request."

I feel his hand on my right thigh. His hand, not the washcloth. That smile is creeping back onto his lips. He doesn't have to ask me anything. I bend my leg and open myself up to him. He caresses my inner thigh in soft, slow massages. I sigh and sink further into the water.

His fingers caress my lips. I jerk violently as a lightning bolt shoots through me.

"You are more sensitive today," he says, his fingers circling my clit.

"Yes, but you can still tease me," I sigh, blinking up at him.

"Whatever you want," he says, dancing his fingertips across from my clit down to my opening.

I lift both legs over the sides of the tub, wantonly splaying my thighs and dumping a bunch of water onto Salvatore and the bathroom floor.

"I wanted to be discreet," he says, lifting on his knees to hover over me.

"No, thank you. Oh, God, right there."

Salvatore cradles my head in his arm and smooths his knuckles across my cheek, teasing my opening with tight circles and pressure as if he's about to push one of his thick fingers inside of me, but he doesn't.

"Please." The shudder that wracks through my body makes that one word at least half a dozen desperate syllables.

He moves until the tips of our noses are touching, his fingers grazing my chin and down my neck.

"This is what you wanted," he says.

"Asshole," I laugh and then gasp when Salvatore pushes his fingers roughly between my ass cheeks.

"Here, bella?"

He'll have to answer that question on his own because I'm too busy humping against his wrist, needing to get any friction against my clit that I can. I just want to come.

I *need* to come.

"Touch yourself, Shae."

He doesn't need to tell me that twice. Hell, I'm mad I didn't think of it myself.

I grab my left breast with one hand and circle my clit with the other. My body seizes in pleasure. I stop breathing. I stop thinking.

Salvatore begins to push one finger into my asshole, gentle and steady, carefully as if he's afraid I'll break.

"I'll be careful now, so you'll know that I can be careful later. Just relax and let me in."

"Fffuck." That word shimmers and shivers as much from the gentle burn of his intrusion as his promise.

I slow the circles on my clit until he's buried his middle finger deep inside my ass. "I...I've never. Holy shit."

Salvatore kisses me on my cheek, the tip of my nose, and the point of my chin while he hooks his thumb into my pussy.

I stroke my clit faster.

He kisses his way down my throat and chest and then laves my hard nipple while he moves his fingers inside me. "Help me," he whispers against my breast, his breath ghosting over my hand. "Help me get you off."

My hand is moving so fast that I'm splashing water all over the place. It takes a while for Salvatore to almost catch up to me, caressing my perineum with his fingers, a kind of pleasure I hadn't even known was possible. Salvatore's elegant pajamas are soaked. He's leaned over into the bathtub to lick and suck and gently bite my nipple.

"I...I..."

He mumbles something, but his mouth is too full of my breast.

I let him have the rest of my flesh and wrap my arm around his head, burying my face in his hair.

"Fuck, I'm coming! I love you," I scream as all the muscles in my body lock, and I come so hard I know this can't be a dream.

Even though every moment with Salvatore feels like one.

I don't believe in luck, and I don't believe in God, but I know it can't be anything other than divine intervention that gives me an uninterrupted morning with Shae. By the time Pedro arrives to fetch me, I've made Shae come with my hands and mouth, showered, and put on the same outfit from yesterday.

"I don't—" Shae says while gripping the front of my shirt.

"I know. I know." It takes a while to pry her hands from my clothes, but I don't rush her. I don't care if Pedro has to wait or if The Board becomes agitated; Shae is all that matters. I kiss the knuckles on each of her delicate hands and then smooth a knuckle over her cheek. "I will be fine."

I watch as she bravely swallows her fear, looks up at me with tears shimmering in her eyes, and lifts onto the balls of her feet to kiss me hard and fast. "Promise?" she mumbles against my lips.

"Promise."

"She is beautiful, Salvatore," Pedro says.

I wait until the door is closed behind the last guard before I grab Pedro by the collar of his jacket. He's not a small man, but I am so full of rage that he feels like nothing when I slam him against the wall and lift him into the air.

"If you mention her again — if you *look* at her again — I'll make sure that you spend the rest of your days, however short, breathing, eating, and shitting through tubes." I say these words in a calm voice. My father always told me that the best threats are quiet; the most dangerous men move in shadow. He might not have taken his own advice seriously, but I did.

I do.

Pedro has a sick smile on his face. "Eccoti, Salvatore. Il Macellaio."

It doesn't sting to hear my old nickname. I've never run from it. And if people remember me as I once was, hopefully they remember the consequences of angering me.

"Do you hear me?" I ask Pedro, still holding him in the air.

"Si, padrino."

I let him down and then straighten his shirt. "Good. Please, lead the way."

"Si, padrino."

Pedro leads me to a room at the heart of the villa.

Alfonso and Giulio think in terms of conflict only, physical and mental, and they view this room as just another ring for battle. They are not wrong. Every time I have been called to this room, it has been to witness someone fight for their life with words and, more often than not, lose. I refuse to let that be my — and Shae's — fate.

But I'm certain the other men I saw in this predicament thought the same.

"Arrivati," Pedro says in a bright tone as if he's a waiter leading me to my table. I would love to say that the pleasure he takes in this macabre presentation terrifies me, but it doesn't.

This is my world.

This is where I belong.

I incline my head to Pedro as I walk past him into a long boardroom with a table specifically made to fit the full Board, which is comprised of a Don from every region of the country. While they're in this room, they only refer to one another by their regions, but I know their names. I know each of these men by sight, and I memorized their biographies years ago, at first out of anger and then as a sound business strategy.

They are all here. Save one. But they have a quorum, and that means this meeting is serious.

I can only assume that Flavia is laughing from hell.

"Have a seat, Salvo," Piemonte says, pointing toward the head of the long table on the other side of the room from the door.

There's an empty chair in front of me, but no one ever sits there. Only a fool would put their back to the door. Besides, if I sat there, the dons wouldn't get the pleasure of sitting in pure silence while I walk the full length of the room to the other chair.

It's the smallest, pettiest display of their power. I've seen some men flinch at just this part, but I would never, especially not when I spot the man sitting in a chair on the side of the room — a place where I have sat, waiting silently until I was called to give The Board the information they needed to pass judgment.

Aldo Milanese is grinning at me like a child waiting for a treat. I've seen this look from him before, but I remind myself that he's not a predator. He's a bottom feeder, which holds its own kind of danger, but a predator he is not.

I'm the predator here, and I can tell which of the men around the table remember that and which ones think I have gone soft with age like them.

I sit slowly in the empty chair at the head of the table, facing the door. "Capi," I say with a respectful tip of my head.

"We received a request," Sardinia says.

"Two requests," Liguria corrects, never missing a moment to argue with Sardinia.

"We'll deal with them one at a time," Abruzzo says, raising his voice just above respectful. He's the youngest man on The Board and still deferential to the older capos, even when they're behaving like children.

I let my gaze move around the table, never letting my

eyes stop for too long on one face. "As you wish. Where would you like to begin?"

Piemonte turns and nods to Aldo. He stands quickly — too eager, childish.

"Capi," he says. "Thank you for your time."

"Get on with it," Puglia says irritably.

I glance at the old man who always seems to have aged twenty years since I saw him last. His hair used to be a full chestnut mop on his head, always disheveled, but now his round head is completely bald and covered with dark brown spots, more each time I see him. His face is deep-set with wrinkles, his mouth is slack and wet, and his small eyes are closed as they often are these days. The rumor is that he's blind, but no one knows for sure. It's been years, but in my mind, I can still see him with a mirthless smile on his face, reclining in the back seat of my father's car.

"Si, si," Aldo says, his giddy smile gone when I turn back to him. He reaches carefully into his jacket pocket and pulls out a thick envelope. "Two months ago, I received a letter in the mail from Salvatore's wife."

"Flavia Torrino is more than 'Salvatore's wife.' Her father was a great man," Puglia says, spitting those words out like a curse.

I don't bother looking in his direction, but I rest my chin in my hand and cover my mouth with my fingers. This is not the time to be found smiling.

"Scuse, capo, si. I received a letter accusing Salvatore of making plans on my territory."

"And what did you do with that information?" I ask.

Molise curses at me to hold my tongue, and I nod my head in simple apology. He turns to Aldo. "What did you do with that information?"

I don't plan to die here today, but if I do, watching Aldo squirm at that question is a sliver of happiness I will take to my grave if this is the end, and even if it is not.

"Capi, I-I know that I should have brought this information to you first, but—"

"But you didn't," Abruzzo cuts in, his voice sharp as a knife. "So, what did you do?"

Aldo has recovered himself a bit. "I took measures to protect myself."

"As any man would," Liguria says defensively.

"What he means is that he schemed to have me killed." Aldo's eyes shoot to me, full of anger and fear. "He hired *boys*," I spit that word, "to come at me in the middle of the plaza with police and tourists swarming around. He didn't even have the balls to come to me as a man. Or at least kill me himself."

The men around the table begin to murmur, not because he tried to kill me but because he was reckless and cowardly. What if his men had gotten caught? What if the carabinieri had been able to trace it back to him? To them? To our organization?

Aldo's face has gone red. His forehead is shiny with sweat.

I let him see me smile briefly.

His jaw tics in frustration before he turns back to the table. "Capi, if a man's wife and-and the daughter of a former padrino told you that her husband was coming after you, would you wait? If The Butcher was coming for your head, would you lay down and let him carve you up?"

Even I have to nod at that sound logic. When I turn back to the table, some of the capi are looking at me with clinical precision. I pretend to be contrite, but inside I'm laughing, happy that it was Aldo who reminded them of who I was. They used to call me The Butcher and I'm sure they're all remembering why. A few capi have bent their heads together to confer with their neighbors, but even their eyes stray to me every now and again.

"What do you have to say for yourself, Salvatore?" That question comes from Molise.

"It's untrue."

"Are you calling him a liar?" Puglia spits.

"Yes."

"And Flavia?"

I laugh so hard my shoulders are shaking. "Flavia lied more than she ever told the truth."

Puglia starts to grumble, but Sardinia cuts him off. "Lied?"

I nod. "Flavia spent a year trying to kill me. When I found out about it, I tried to neutralize her, only to find out that this," I say, gesturing dismissively in Aldo's direction, "was her contingency plan. She was her father's daughter. So, I handled her the way I handled him."

The grumbling is much louder now.

"Kill him," someone mutters under their breath.

Coward.

"Do you have proof that she tried to kill you?" Abruzzo asks.

"If you need it," I say with a shrug. "But if I didn't kill her after we married, what would make me do so now?"

"Good question," some of the capi mutter begrudgingly. I can't count them all, but I know Calabria, Marche, and Umbria are part of the chorus.

"Maybe we should consider your request now," Abruzzo says. "You want to leave."

"I do. So, I certainly don't need more territory." I spare a withering glance at Aldo.

"Why now?"

I drop my hands to my lap, and now my back does tighten. I'm afraid to even think of Shae in this room, but I cannot avoid her no matter how hard I try. "I met a woman I do not deserve." I don't avert my gaze from the table; that would be a sign of weakness, and I won't give any of these men the pleasure.

"A woman?" someone asks in disbelief.

"I don't understand," one of the other capos says.

Aldo cuts in. "He's running. He's been caught out, and he's trying to escape punishment."

I roll my eyes. "The only way out, normally, is death. Think before you speak."

A few of the capi chuckle lightly. Embarrassment and anger bunch Aldo's features. If only he would learn from this shame before it's too late.

"Explain yourself," Liguria says.

I don't want to. I shouldn't have to. But life, especially this life, is not fair. It does not respect boundaries, privacy, or trauma. This Board is the thief of time and joy. And I won't subject Shae and our child to that.

"Many of you knew my father." I let that sentence stand on its own for a few moments. I look around the room again, and this time, I allow my gaze to linger. I look each of the men who knew my father well enough to have him killed in the eye. So many are dead — I killed the man who pulled the trigger before I married his daughter, the ones who helped dispose of his body died one by one years before that — but the men who ordered the hit are all here in front of me.

"My father was killed before he saw me become a man. He didn't get to say goodbye to my mother. He never got to set his life in order."

"Salvo," someone says, and I hold up my hands.

"Flavia always knew her father's death was a possibility. She hated me for being the one who killed him, but she knew it would happen one day. But Shae—" Her name is like velvet fire on my tongue. "She doesn't know this life. I don't want it for her."

"So you'll give it up? For a woman?" Abruzzo asks, his tone light with something that sounds like a blend of awe and disbelief.

"In a heartbeat," I say, thinking of hearing our child's heartbeat one day. I'll give all this up for *that* heartbeat.

"What will you do?" Molise asks gently, which is far more shocking than anything else I've heard here today.

I shrug and smile. "Whatever she wants."

"Where will you go?" Puglia spits.

I look at his still-shuttered face. "America." Only I see that small twitch in his right cheek.

"The only way out is death," Aldo says, trying to remind The Board of their own ancient rules. But his voice is a plaintive whine, and I watch as men who hate and fear me cut their eyes in his direction.

Aldo never did know when to shut up.

"The woman is here," Abruzzo says. "We took her with Salvatore as leverage. Whatever we decide to do with him, she will leave here unmolested."

"I agree," Molise says.

The table erupts in deliberation, but they all agree to that in the end and I sigh in relief.

"You can't be thinking of letting him go."

I sigh again, but this time in deep irritation at Aldo's whining. A number of the capi join me to Aldo's great distress.

"Someone call Pedro," Liguria starts, but just then, the door bursts open, and Pedro walks into the room.

There's a playful smile on the man's face and a gun trained at the back of his head.

WITHOUT SALVATORE, I decide that being kidnapped is boring.

I mean, I'm still scared, but after a relatively good night's sleep and a few orgasms, I find that it's actually hard to hold onto the fear. Maybe it's the surroundings — there's not even a television in the room! — and my absent cell phone — I haven't even *thought* about my cell phone in days!

But now that I'm alone, all I can think about is all the other shit I could be doing. Like Salvatore, for instance!

I also might be making my life harder because I'm just sitting on the foot of the bed, staring at the door, praying for Salvatore to come back as softly as I can. And I guess because I'm paying such close attention to the door and there's nothing else to make any noise in this room besides my pounding heart, the sound of a commotion in the hallway sounds loud as hell.

Loud and none of my damn business.

I jump up from the bed and sprint toward the bathroom at the sound of someone's — maybe many someones — grunting yells. Sounds like a fight to me, and I kick the bathroom door closed with my left foot. There's nowhere to hide in here, but I lock the door behind me and crouch inside the bathtub in the corner of the room.

I wrap my arms around my stomach and talk to the avocado. "It's okay! We're going to be okay. Your daddy is going to take care of us. And if he fails, Zoe and Zahra will avenge our deaths, probably. And then I guess we'll all be together." I frown and squint at the ceiling as my stomach rumbles. "I didn't even get a last meal!"

Someone shouts in the bedroom. I crouch down as if they can see me. Okay, now there are many people shouting.

"Shae."

I don't recognize the voice, so of course, I don't respond.

It's only when someone tries the doorknob that I realize I should have grabbed something, anything I could use as a weapon.

"Shae, are you in there?"

I gasp. "Lorenzo?!" I shoot up from the bathtub, my foot slips, and I almost faceplant on the tile floor. What a way to damn near kill myself. I cry out.

"Shae!"

Lorenzo starts pounding on the door, but loud, so I assume he's using his shoulder and not his hands.

I hop out of the bathtub. "I'm okay! I almost fell."

The pounding stops. "Open the door."

I'm panting when I turn the doorknob and pull it open.

"Oh my God, you're okay!" I burst into tears and throw my arms around his waist.

"Aww, Lorenzo, you made a friend," Federico teases.

I sigh in relief at the sight of Federico holstering his gun. I see Alfonso standing there, rumpled, breathing heavily, a bead of blood in the corner of his mouth, and I feel safe.

Salvatore sent his army for me.

Giulio

I have a gun in each hand, and my arms are hanging, limp but ready, at my sides. No one knows better than me not to aim a gun until I'm ready to use it, and we're not there yet, I think. But I want to get to the good part. The part that will leave these pistols in my hands hot to the touch. I want this all to be over so I can present Shae to Zahra. So I can keep hold of this fragile new thing we are creating.

I want blood.

Nineteen men around the table. Twenty, including Salvo. Aldo to my right. I don't know how many men are in the building, but I took three out temporarily and one permanently getting into this room. So however many arrived, minus four. Minus Pedro. Minus whoever

Alfonso knocked unconscious just because I didn't tell him to be careful.

I need more information to take stock of the situation as quickly as I can. I can kill half the men in this room on my own right now, but the other half is a mystery. How many are armed? How many are good shots? How long before someone hears the gunshots and comes running? Is Tommaso good with a gun or better with his hands like Alfonso? If Alfonso was here, I'd know our odds — they wouldn't be good, but I'd know them.

"What the fuck is going on?" Tuscany spits. He's aiming the question at Salvo, though, not me.

Good. I need to keep my eyes on Aldo. I know better than most that he doesn't have a problem stabbing a man in the back. It would be my pleasure to put him down.

"Giulio," Salvatore calls. "It is good to see you."

I nod. "I hope I'm not late."

Tuscany slams his fist against the table. "Answer me."

Salvo nods in my direction.

"After the last attempt on your life, I flipped a former poliziotta who says the carabinieri seem to be working with someone to target Salvatore."

"That makes sense," Salvo says, nodding sagely.

"Is that a revelation?" Puglia asks, bored. "When are the carabinieri not aiming for us?"

"Yes, but whoever her boss was working for wasn't interested in bringing down the entire operation. Just Salvo."

The men around the table are quiet as those words sink in. Aldo, however, seems nervous.

"That doesn't mean anything," he says, wiping at his wet forehead.

I glance at Salvo to find him smiling.

"Who's your contact?" Molise asks. Or maybe it's Abruzzo; those two are thick as thieves.

"She was a waitress sent to spy on us. But her boss was named Gallo."

The men around the table grumble in consternation.

"This is pointless," someone says.

"He's just trying to weasel his way out of here," Aldo spits.

"Gallo?" Tommaso asks, so quiet no one but me hears.

Well, no one but me and Carlo.

I step to the side as Carlo turns to Tommaso, shaking his head. "It's not what you think."

"Your family name is Gallo. Your brother works for the carabinieri. Tell me where I'm wrong."

I glance quickly at Salvatore. Some men would gloat at being right. This was the possibility that he'd written in his letter to me. The traitor had to be Tommaso or Carlo; there were no other options, and if he didn't survive this, he told me to kill them both just in case.

"So, it was your brother, Carlo?" Salvatore's voice is uncharacteristically loud, but he needs to cut through the man's sniveling pleas for mercy and remind Tommaso, shocked into silence, that there is still work to be done.

"S-s-si," he says.

"You told him about Flavia?"

Carlo nods.

"And he told you what?"

The room is so quiet that I can hear Carlo's dry gulp. "He didn't tell me anything."

"Why are you looking at him?" Piemonte shouts.

Carlo and Aldo jump.

"If he didn't tell you anything, who did he report to?"

Tommaso is staring a hole into the side of Carlo's face.

"Aldo."

"Figlio di putana!" Tommaso shouts as he twists his body and shifts his gun from the back of Pedro's head to Carlo. The shot hits him dead center in the forehead.

Impressive.

But I'll congratulate him on that shot later; there's still so much work to be done.

"If you take another step, I'll empty this clip into your knees. Happily," I tell Aldo. He's shaking like a leaf, but I watch as thoughts of running away fly from his head.

"I just wanted to protect myself," Aldo says, staring at the barrel of my gun but pleading with The Board.

"Then you defend yourself like a man," Salvatore roars loud enough to make everyone jump, the palm of his hand slamming onto the table.

"Salvo," someone says in a placating tone.

"Shut up," he scowls.

"Who are you speaking to—" Lazio asks, but the rest of that question is drowned out by the boom of a gunshot and the high-pitched wailing of the man as he falls from his chair and crawls away toward death.

Aldo's red face is covered in sweat, and his eyes are

sharp pinpoints of fear. I spare a glance at the conference table. Everyone has turned to stare at Salvatore, his father's Beretta in his hand, a look of contentment softening his face.

"*Now* we can get down to business. Shall we?" he asks, standing from the table.

"Si, padrino," I say happily because I can *finally* do something more than just watch and listen and talk. I fucking hate that.

Salvatore nods at me, and I squeeze the trigger twice.

Aldo crumples to the floor, grabbing his ruined knee. His cries are music to my ears.

Salvatore

Plans change, but ambition never dies, and it's never too late to get revenge.

I stand from the chair, the gurgling sounds of Lazio dying mixing with Aldo's pained cries to create a grating soundtrack at the back of my brain. If I listen too long, they will give me a headache, but I don't plan for this meeting to last long enough for that to happen.

I tuck my chair under the table and cross my hands over the headrest. "Do you know the last thing my father said to me?" I ask. My eyes settle on the gun, heavy and ready for action in my hand. My brain and heart are full of memories of my father cleaning it, a glass of whiskey at hand, a cigarette dangling from his lips.

"He asked you a question," Giulio says calmly. Still, those words are a threat.

"No." I don't have any interest in deciphering who said that. I'm beyond caring.

"I had just gotten in trouble for…something — I was always in trouble. My mother had forbidden me from playing football at the park with my friends for a week. I spent all day waiting for him to arrive because I knew he would override my mother. I *knew* that he would tell her that a boy needed fresh air and football or something." I shrug, remembering that day with the kind of clarity that can only come from grief. "And so, of course, he didn't do that at all. He told me that the sign of a man was the ability to own his mistakes and take responsibility for his actions."

"Your father was a thief."

I know that voice. Sardinia's face is red with rage. At least he doesn't cower when we make eye contact.

"That money should have gone to his padrino," he says. "Every lira he and your uncles kept was one more nail in their coffins. They knew that, and you know that as well."

"You're right." Someone exhales loudly in relief. "I'm not here to avenge my father's honor. I understand exactly who he was."

"Then what is this all about?"

"My mother. My cousins. Me." I punctuate every word by shooting another man in the face. Campania. Piemonte. Veneto. Lombardy. The oldest members of The Board. The five men who were sitting in these seats when The Board decided to have my family members killed; my father and uncle Daniele for their theft, my other uncles as a lesson.

"They knew the consequences, but the coffins they constructed..." I shake my head in grief. "We never got the chance to bury them. That was on your orders, Milo, yes?" I aim this question at Sardinia. He hadn't been a capo then, not even a padrino, just another soldier trying to make a name for himself. And he did — by helping to kill my father and uncles.

"The Board said they needed to be eliminated, but it was you who made sure there was nothing to find, right? Nothing for their families to bury?"

"I won't apologize for doing my job."

"I'd never ask you to do that. But you can take respon-sibility, can't you, Milo?"

The men around the table start to grumble. "We don't use names in this room," Pedro says.

I turn, surprised to see that Tommaso still has a gun aimed at his head. "I forgot you were here."

Pedro shrugs. "Thank you."

I turn back to Sardinia. "Where were we?"

"If I tell you—"

I shake my head and cluck my tongue. "*When* you tell me."

"Will you kill me?"

I scratch at my beard. "No. If you tell me that it was you, I'll beat you to within an inch of your life, but I will let you live."

"It was me."

I aim my gun directly at his face.

His eyes narrow to slits. "You said you wouldn't kill me."

"And you said you understood that there are consequences for your actions." I squeeze the trigger just as he curses at me.

I look at the six men slumped over in their chairs and sigh in relief.

For years I dreamed about what it would feel like to make it to this moment. I thought I would feel happy, but I just feel...complete. I've been waiting decades for this moment, and now it's done.

"What now, Sasà?"

My jaw tics. No one has called me that name in decades. When I turn to Puglia — Andrea — one of my father's closest friends, his eyes are open. They've gone watery and pale with age, but they're still as warm as I remember.

"I don't know."

"Bullshit," Andrea says with a laugh. "You know. You still want to leave?"

My eyes flit around the room to Giulio and Tommaso, their guns still steady. I take in what's left of The Board. I think of Shae.

"Yes," I say without hesitation. "Shae wants to go home, and I want to be with her."

Andrea laughs. "Then you go. You deserve a rest."

"A rest?"

"Si, si, but *only* a rest. Pedro," Andrea calls. The other man walks away from Tommaso's gun without a care in the world. "Take some time. Do some research. And then we can begin again. There is still so much work to be done. Work your father started, and now we get to finish."

"Andrea," I groan.

He stands from the table slowly, batting his name away. "Before you go, you will need to name your successor."

"Andrea."

Pedro says something to the old man.

"I was wondering why Luca was not here!" Andrea's laughter sounds exactly how I remember it. "I've been waiting years for that. Don't worry. I already have someone in mind. Tommaso, I am sorry for your loss. Let us have a chat."

I watch in shock as Andrea, Pedro, and Tommaso walk slowly from the room.

I shake my head and look at Giulio.

Abruzzo clears his throat to get my attention. "Are you done?"

"Oh, yes. Thank you," I say, holding my father's gun in the air. I don't know how he got it into this room; all that matters is that it was here when I needed it. "Does this mean we have a deal?"

Abruzzo and Molise stand at the same time.

"We have our own reasons for supporting you here," Molise says.

"I'm sure."

"But yes," Abruzzo adds. "We have a deal. And you know Andrea is the head of The Board now?"

I sigh in exasperation. "I know."

"Was that your plan?"

I think back to the message Andrea somehow left in my office days ago. I don't know how, and Andrea has never been a man to share his secrets. Not even with me. "Not exactly," I say. "I just knew that I needed all the allies I could get."

"True. He is right, you know. You will need to choose your successor and appoint your proxy."

"Proxy?"

"For The Board. You're a don now."

"Welcome," Molise says, a wry smile on his face.

"Does it never fucking end?" I groan, glancing toward Giulio, who will not be happy with me soon.

"No," Molise says, and the two of them walk slowly from the room, with the last of The Board rushing after them.

When it's just Giulio, Aldo, and I, Giulio finally drops his arm.

"What do you want me to do about him?"

"Where is Shae?"

"With Alfonso, Lorenzo, and Federico waiting for us."

"Waiting?"

He rolls his eyes. "If she's anything like Zahra, I thought she wouldn't leave here without you. Anyway, Federico looked like he'd rip anyone who got too close to her into small pieces. So, I assume she's safe."

She might be safe, but I need to see that for myself. I rush around the table toward the door.

"Salvo," Giulio calls. "What do you want me to do about Aldo?"

"Whatever you want," I call over my shoulder.

The gunshot rings out before I can finish that sentence. It looks like I wasn't the only one who got some justice today.

I DON'T LET Salvatore out of my sight for the next two days.

Or he doesn't let me out of his sight. Whatever, the tenor of our relationship after we get back to the penthouse is co-dependency, but I think that's temporarily okay. I mean, we *were* kidnapped. Besides that, though, the next couple of days are frustratingly normal. Salvatore cooks for us. We sleep. We fuck. He washes my back. I hear my cousins arguing outside of the door sometimes, wanting to see me. But besides our quick family reunion when they brought me back from the villa, I don't have the energy to talk to anyone but him, and he takes the blame with my cousins.

Although, truth be told, we don't talk nearly as much as we should. I just want to rest.

Until this afternoon, when I woke up from my post-breakfast orgasm-induced nap and needed to speak to someone in particular.

"Hello."

"Auntie Caroline, this is a FaceTime. Do you have the phone up to your ear?"

"A what time?" she asks.

"Put the phone in front of you and look at the screen."

I wait for a few seconds until her face comes into view. "Move the phone back just a little bit."

She does, and I see her squinting at me. "Hey! There you are! Where are my glasses?" Once her attention wavers, her hand dips, and I have a great view of her chin.

"They're on your head, auntie."

"Huh? Oh. Oh!" She comes back into view. "Alright," she sighs. "That's better. Well, look at you! Have you called your mother?"

"No, ma'am. Not yet."

"But you found your cousin?"

"Oh, yes! We did!" There's no need to tell her we found Zahra almost immediately. What the Council don't know won't hurt 'em.

"Well, good. You coulda told us," she mutters. "But I'll let the other aunts know. So, when are you coming back?"

"Um...soon. Soon. That's actually why I'm calling."

"Oh, the ticket is open-ended. All you gotta do is call the airline. But I can do that for you if you want. Just tell me when you three are coming back."

"No, not that. Um..."

Caroline stares intently at me, and it doesn't matter that there's thousands of miles between us; I feel her gaze, and I know what she's waiting to hear. This is the reason I called her.

"I'm pregnant," I admit in a quiet voice.

"Well, duh, girl. We'll talk about the baby shower when you're back. We're gon' have to find you somewhere else to stay, though. Ain't no way Zoe's gonna want to live with a newborn. Oh, it's not Steve's, is it?" Caroline's frown is excellent.

"No, auntie."

"Oh, good. 'Cause girl..."

"I know, auntie."

"So...who is the father?"

"That's also why I'm calling."

"Oh? Did you find something else while you were looking for Zahra? An Italian noodle?" she asks, echoing auntie Mina.

I laugh so hard there are tears in my eyes.

"Oooh, looks like you did."

The bedroom door opens, and Salvatore peeks his head inside.

"Bella, are you awake?"

Caroline cackles.

Salvatore looks at me in confusion.

"I'm talking to my aunt."

"Okay," he says and begins to back out.

"Wait," I call.

Caroline is still laughing.

"Do you want... Do you want to meet her?"

"Yes, bella. Of course." He walks into the room and

actually runs a hand through his hair and straightens the glasses on his face.

"You look great," I say wistfully.

"Oh, somebody caught some feelings," Caroline laughs.

Salvatore sits on the bed and throws his arm around my waist. He kisses my cheek, and then I turn the phone toward us.

Caroline stops laughing, and she brings her phone closer to her face. "Girl, get your big ole head out the way so I can see him up close."

"My head's not that big," I grumble, shoving the phone into Salvatore's hand.

"Salvatore, this is my aunt Caroline. Caroline, this is Salvatore. The father of my baby."

As soon as I say the word 'baby,' he starts to smile. "Ciao, Caroline."

"Well, hello there, Salvatore. Are you taking care of my niece?"

His smile falters as he turns to me. "With everything I have, I'm trying."

"He is. You are."

This is why we aren't talking as much as we definitely should. I can feel his guilt, and he can probably feel my lingering fear. There is so much that we will have to work through.

"And are you married or otherwise attached?" Caroline asks, not bothering to let us process these emotions on her time.

"No," he says. "I'm a widower, actually."

"I'm sorry to hear that."

"Don't be," he says resolutely.

I didn't think this through. We needed more time to figure out a cover story. Or I needed more time to explain to Salvatore exactly how much truth we could tell my family and set up the lies. Too late now.

"It was not a happy marriage," he says far too earnestly.

Caroline shrugs. "Been there. And are you financially capable of caring for this new life you two are bringing into the world? Because we love Shae, but Lord knows money has not been her focus."

"Auntie Caroline?"

"Taking care of Shae and our children is all that matters. She will never want for anything from here on out."

Caroline squints at the phone for a few seconds and smiles. "Good, good. Make sure you say exactly that when you meet the rest of the family. And if you can make the accent just a little bit thicker—"

"Okay, Auntie Caroline, that's enough." I snatch the phone from his hand and frown — respectfully — at the screen.

"Well, alright, you have a good time for the rest of your trip. Make sure you let your mama know when you're coming back."

I sigh. "Yes, ma'am."

"And will you be coming back with her, Salvatore?"

He squeezes my waist. "Yes. Wherever she goes, I will be there."

"Ooh, that's a good one. Keep that one in your back pocket. Bye now."

There are a few seconds where Caroline is frowning at her cell phone before she hangs up. Salvatore and I sit through that silently.

"I think that went very well," he says.

I can't help but smile. "That's adorable. I'm going to have to prepare you for meeting the family, and first of all, do *not* tell Caroline anything you don't want the rest of the family to know."

"Like what?"

"Like about your wife," I whisper. "You shouldn't have told her that."

"We should not lie about things that can be verified by a lawyer."

"Oh. Good point. But you also should be careful about details." He squints at me. "Children. You said *children*."

"Do you no longer want more than one child?"

"Of course not. I want all the babies. But my family is going to start thinking that you just got with me because I'm young and fertile."

He smiles. "Well, that wasn't the intention, but now that you mention it..." He crawls onto his knees and pushes me back onto the bed.

"Oh my God," I laugh at him. "Oh my God," I groan as his fingers get started on my post-nap pre-lunch orgasm.

"Well, look who's alive," Zoe says as soon as I walk out of the condo building's front door. She's waiting there with Zahra and the rest of Salvatore's men, who aren't even trying to hide that they're on bodyguard duty.

"And glowing," Zahra adds.

Salvatore squeezes my hand and kisses my temple.

"How cute," Zoe says, snatching me out of Salvatore's hold. Zahra grabs the hand he reluctantly releases, and we start walking down the street with Lorenzo leading the way. His head is swiveling left and right, his hand never far from the gun holster I can just about see through his suit jacket now that I know what I'm looking for. He's been hovering close since we got back from the villa as well.

I wonder what will happen to him and Federico when we leave, but my cousins don't give me time to ponder that.

"So, Giulio says you and Sal are going back to the States," Zahra says.

I nod. "We're going to stop in Rome and Naples on the way but yeah. I want to raise the baby near family, and he doesn't have any family here. I mean, besides these guys."

I look over my shoulder and see Salvatore walking between Giulio and Alfonso, Federico and Manuele and some of his other men helicoptering around them protectively.

"They are his family, huh?"

"Definitely," Zoe says. "I mean, in a strange way."

"Not so strange now," Zahra adds. "For Giulio and Alfonso, I mean. Because they're with us."

I squint at her, and then my mouth falls open. "Zoe Christine, what the fuck did I miss?"

"Not you using my first and middle! But a lady never tells," she says, lifting her nose in the air.

"You sure? Because I distinctly remember a very long and needlessly detailed story about anal sex that I didn't even ask for, *lady*." Zahra puts extra emphasis on that last word.

"That was purely educational," Zoe says, smiling.

"Well, educate me on what happened between you and Alfonso," I practically scream.

"Happen*ing*," Zahra says. "We ran into them in the elevator last night and saw a *lot* more than we asked for."

"Zoe, oh my God."

"Calm down," Zoe says. "No need to break my eardrums. All I will say is that Alfonso and I enjoy each other's company, and we will be continuing to do so for the time being."

This is music to Zahra's ears, apparently, because she throws her head back to laugh.

My cousin's words sting. "So, you— You're staying in Italy?"

Zoe finally looks at me again as Zahra's laughter fades away. "Yeah. I am. I'm just not ready to leave yet."

"What about your job?"

Zoe shrugs. "Alfonso's entire family is here, and I can do my job anywhere. My editor is salivating at me being based in Europe for a while." She shrugs again, but this time, the smile is returning to her face. "Apparently, the only thing keeping me back home was my last relationship and my apartment. And since you're going back, you and Sal can stay there as long as you need."

I sigh, wanting to say something, but there's nothing to say, not really. I can't ask Zoe to come back to the States with me just because I want her to. We tried and failed with Zahra, and all those defenses still stand.

I turn to my other cousin. She's beaming at me, not to rub it in but because she's happy. "I'm still staying," she says, even though I didn't ask. "Giulio's taking over for Sal. We're going to look for a new apartment together. I'm eating my way through Italian pastries and desserts."

"Are you going to work here?" Zoe asks.

"Nah. I'm very into the kept woman's life of lust and leisure."

"Oh, bitch, that's a title. You should write a book," Zoe says.

"Maybe I will. And since you're going to be very close by, you can help."

"Or not. But if you're good, I'll convince Alfonso to invite you to Positano for research. His brother has a boat."

"Deal!" Zahra squeals.

"Yay, and since we're agreeing…"

"Here we go," Zahra mutters under her breath.

"I need you to convince Giulio to give Alfonso a week's vacation."

"Did he ask?"

"No, because he's very sweet. I am not. We're still

getting to know each other, and I would like to do that without you two around for a while."

"She means she wants to send us away so they can get freaky without running into us," Zahra whispers to me.

"Yes, exactly," Zoe agrees.

Zahra shrugs. "Okay. But only because he's good for you."

"Not this again," Zoe groans in irritation.

I listen to them trade sisterly barbs back and forth over my head, feeling sadder by the moment.

And then Zoe squeezes my arm. "Hey."

I look at her, shake my head, and smile. "I'm okay," I say, those words undercut by the wobbly sound of my voice and the tear that slips from the corner of my eye.

"Don't cry!" Zahra screeches.

"Aw, Shae Butter," Zoe says, hugging me. "Don't be sad. Everything is going to be fine."

"Is it? You're going to be here, and I'm going to be at home. Oh, God, I'm going to have to explain to the Council that I lost both of you here."

"Nah, you're good on that. I've been writing an email. I'll send it when you leave."

"Is it rude?" Zahra asks.

"No, I'm not a heathen. I love those weird old women."

"Okay, let me read over it, and if it's not terrible, I'll sign it."

"Write your own letter, mooch."

Zahra sucks her teeth.

"Anyway," Zoe says, turning back to me. "From what

I can gather, your man is leaving but still very much in the mix, so I don't think this is going to be your last trip to Italy."

"At all. And, of course, I will be coming home for every Thanksgiving. Something tells me I will not be able to get mama's dressing in Naples."

"Girl!" Zoe agrees. "We'll also come home for weddings and funerals and Shae Butter Baby's first birthday."

"Oh, we are definitely calling the baby that. Lemme text Symone."

My eyes go wide. "Um, does Symone know I'm pregnant?"

"Yeah, apparently, auntie Caroline has been telling everyone since the summer," Zahra says, texting quickly with her thumb.

"What?"

"Girl, please, she's been dreaming about fish for months," Zoe says. "She thought it was you or Symone, but then she ran into Symone at Costco with an industrial-sized box of tampons."

I'm shocked. But not surprised.

"Done," Zahra says. "Look, the point is that we love you."

"Very much."

"And nothing is going to keep us from you or this baby."

"I... I know that, but..." I'm overcome with so much emotion that I can't finish that sentence.

Thankfully, my cousins know what I mean and how I

feel. Zoe kisses my cheek while Zahra grabs my hand again. We're walking practically hip to hip. I don't know when this will happen again, so I decide, like I have so many times this year, to just enjoy every moment I can spend with these people I love.

"You know, maybe I should write a novel instead of a memoir," Zahra says out of the blue. "Because who the hell is going to believe this weird ass story!"

We burst into laughter at this.

"What's so funny?" Alfonso asks as the men catch up with us.

We'll have to tell them later. We're far too busy holding onto one another and laughing until tears are running down our cheeks.

I'll miss this most of all.

"How do I look?" Shae asks me for the third time since we left Zoe's apartment.

"Beautiful," I tell her as I have each time.

We're walking down a quiet residential street because Shae wanted to walk to the meeting with her aunts, and I cannot say no to her. No one can. Lorenzo would always prefer that Shae travel by car, and Federico hates the biting wind, but what Shae wants, Shae gets. I often wonder who those two are more devoted to, Shae or myself. I know which I prefer, and so do they.

"You always say I look beautiful."

"You always look beautiful."

She rolls her eyes and smiles. "Thank you. But do I look like I let a strange older man knock me up the day we met?"

"Strange?" I gasp.

"Okay, foreign, but I mean..." She stops walking and turns in a circle, the skirt of her dress fanning out and exposing her bare thighs even though it's getting far too cold for that.

I lick my lips and then smile as the dress settles over her rounded belly, still small, but definitely there.

She's panting lightly when she stops. "I'm just wondering if this dress says, 'I'm your respectable daughter who would never let my new boyfriend come in me right after doing some illegal things we don't talk about.'"

"That is a lot to ask a dress to communicate." I'm trying not to laugh, but the sight of Federico barely holding back his own laughter over Shae's shoulder makes it harder to hold it in.

"I should have asked Zahra. She was always so good at putting her best face forward with the Aunties."

"Bella." I pull her to me, planting small kisses over her face until she smiles and opens her mouth to me.

This is the life I wanted, the life I gladly left Italy to protect. A life where Shae thinks of some new part of the city she wants to show me. Where I wake up every day with her in my arms. Where I spend every afternoon buried to the hilt inside her cunt. A life we get to build together, piece by piece.

This is the honeymoon period. Soon enough, Andrea will call me, and it will be time to get back to work. Our baby will arrive, and we will not have so many hours of freedom together. But even those moments will be all the sweeter because they will be ours. Shae and I will have the life we chose together, and since the day I met her, this has been my only dream.

"I don't want to give them any reason not to like you."

"You cannot control that." I brush her cheek with my knuckles. "And they love you. If they're anything like your cousins, they will tolerate me for that alone."

She purses her lips. "I...guess that's true."

"And even if they don't like me now, they will come around."

"You don't know that."

I kiss her quickly. "True, but I think when they see how happy I make you..." I lift my eyebrows in a silent question.

"Oh, very happy," she laughs, nodding excitedly.

"Once they see that, I think they will. And if they don't, that is also okay."

She shakes her head.

"It is, bella. You do not have to make everyone happy. You could not if you tried." Her body tenses against me. "But you do not need to try to make me happy. Every minute with you is better than the last. Every day with you is my dream come true."

Her eyes begin to water. "I really love you," she whispers.

"Ti amo tanto. And once we are done here, I will remind you just how much."

Her eyes soften like molten brown lava. "Yeah?"

"Si."

"Shae, hurry up!"

We both frown and turn to see a woman standing in front of a building down the street.

"Who is that?"

Shae sighs. "My cousin Symone. The Aunties must have sent her because we're late."

"We aren't late."

Shae sighs and pulls out of my grasp. "Auntie Pearl says being early is on time, being on time is late, and being late is uncouth."

"I—"

She grabs my hand and pulls me forward. "Don't worry, babe. You'll get the hang of their quirks eventually."

We rush the rest of the way down the street.

"Hey, Symone," Shae waves.

Symone frowns at Lorenzo in what looks like confusion before turning to Shae with a smile. "Hey! Welcome home."

"Thanks. What's the mood up there?"

Symone smiles. "I think you're good, but Zoe told me to tell you if you think things are going south, just put your hand over your stomach and remind them you're pregnant. You know how they are about shit like that."

"Oh, that's smart."

Symone nods quickly. "Um...who are these guys?"

Shae looks at me with wide eyes. "Friends," I lie easily.

Symone blinks slowly. "Sure. They can come in the apartment, but not in the room when you meet with the aunts."

Federico starts to say something, but I hold up my hand. "That is acceptable."

"Great accent. Can you make it thicker?"

I smile. "I can see the family resemblance now."

That seems to be the exact compliment Symone wanted to hear. She stands up straighter and beams at us. "Thanks. He'll be good. Let's go."

Symone turns on the point of her feet and leads us into the building. "*We* will be fantastic," I tell Shae.

She kisses me and covers her stomach with her free hand. "If things go south, just start speaking in Italian," she whispers.

Shae

I am a fully grown adult. I am.

But sitting in front of the Council of Aunties always makes me feel like a kid. Or guilty. And I'm neither of those things this time! Innocence doesn't alleviate the phantom guilt, unfortunately.

"Well, then," great-great-aunt Mina says, sitting imperiously in her chair, looking vaguely in our direction. "Someone tell me what he looks like."

"He's white," someone says.

"Well, she did bring him back from Italy," another auntie says in my defense.

"There are Black people in Italy," I say. I've been doing some research.

"Did you think about bringing one of them home, sweetheart?" auntie Mildred asks.

"Love is love," my mother says. "Isn't that what the kids say?"

"Mama, when have you ever heard me say that?"

My mother throws her hands up in exasperation. "Well, somebody said it."

"Is 'white' all y'all got? Lord, let me use my imagination. But after that other sad white boy she was dating, I hate to say it, but I don't have much hope."

"Auntie Mina?" I whine.

"Oh, no judgment, honey. We like what we like."

"How is that not the same thing I just said?" mama cries.

"Lord, please end my suffering today."

"Don't take the Lord's name in vain," Nana Geraldine chides me.

"Sorry," I mumble, feeling younger every moment.

I steal a peak at Salvatore, and he seems...ecstatic. "Why are you smiling?" I ask.

He squeezes the hand he's holding in his lap. "How could I not? Your family is wonderful."

"What?" I shriek.

"What? I have faced worse," he says nonchalantly.

"We'll see about that," auntie Mildred says, eyeing me through her glasses with a hard frown.

He wipes the smile from his face, but I can still feel his glee at this spectacle. I cannot understand it, but I think it's going to take more than auntie Mildred's stare or auntie Mina's interjections to strip him of his excitement.

I guess I'm going to have to shoulder all this embarrassment on my own.

"Auntie—"

Mildred holds up her hand to silence me. "I sent you and Zoe to Italy, but only you returned."

I open my mouth to defend myself, but Zoe and Zahra's mother steps in to save me. "I've talked to my girls," she says. "We can handle them at a different meeting. But they are happy and healthy, and their decisions aren't Shae's responsibility."

The Council nods in agreement.

"Okay, then let's deal with the matter at hand," Mildred says, turning to Salvatore. She looks him over silently. The entire Council does.

Steve didn't even make it to this formal introduction; if he had, he would have fallen apart. But Salvatore soaks up their attention. He crosses his legs and smiles at the Aunties before lifting my hand to kiss his mouth.

"Oh, this is a smooth one, Mina," Nana Geraldine says.

"Like smoother than her last one? 'Cause that wouldn't be that damn hard."

"No, no. He's smooth. I bet he swept her off her feet."

"Oh," Mina laughs. "She needs that."

"I am *right* here?" I say into the void of their chatter.

"Where else would you be?" my mother asks. "And hush, girl."

"Caroline says you're pregnant," Mildred says.

"Yes, ma'am."

"And you're keeping this baby?"

"Yes," Salvatore and I say in unison.

"And you can afford that?" Mina asks. "Ain't nothing worse than a broke man."

"You sure about that?" someone asks, echoing my own thoughts.

"Well," Mina laughs, "I guess there are a few things that might be worse."

I shake my head. Salvatore chuckles lightly.

"Yes," he says. "Shae will want for nothing for the rest of her life, and neither will our children."

"So you do want more kids?" Mildred asks me.

"Yes," I answer eagerly. "Definitely."

My mother is preening like I just won the Nobel Peace Prize or something, and I sigh in exasperation. Child or not, I'm over this.

"Is that it?" I ask irritably.

"Shae," my mother warns.

I lock eyes with Mildred. "I don't have to justify my decisions to the Council."

"Oop, somebody came back with a backbone," Mina laughs. "Maybe we should send all the meek ones to Italy."

"That would be nice," Salvatore says, kissing my hand and winking at me.

I have to bite back a smile, but I don't back down. "Salvatore and I are together. We're going to have this baby. And I won't be back to this Council to explain myself again."

Someone in the back of the room snaps.

"We'll see," Mildred says, a smile on her face. "Don't

get too big for your britches."

"In a few months, she won't be able to fit those britches anyway," Nana Geraldine says, and the entire Council laughs.

I look at Salvatore and smile at him.

"What are britches?" he asks.

The Aunties laugh louder, and even I manage a smile, but only briefly. I stand from my chair and pull Salvatore up with me.

I don't know how it's possible for the entire Council to make me feel so small while looking *up* at me. Maybe that's a skill they learned with age. But I refuse to be cowed by them right now.

"I love you all, but if there are no more pressing questions, we're going to go."

I wait two seconds, and when no one says anything, I head for the door.

"Ciao, zie!" Salvatore says companionably. "I look forward to getting to know you all."

"Oh, he is smooth," Mina says.

My hand closes on the door handle, and my mother's voice stops me in my tracks. "We're having dinner at my house tomorrow. Your father wanted some étouffée. Can I expect you two to be there?"

My stomach growls at the word 'étouffée.' "What time?" I ask without turning around.

"Six."

"Should we bring anything?"

"You don't have to," my mother says, not meaning a word of that.

"Of course, we will bring something," Salvatore says quickly. The Aunties eat that up.

I sigh. "See you there."

"Mmmhmm," the entire Council says as one.

I push the door open and rush out into the hallway.

We walk back to the living room. Symone is sitting on the plastic-covered couch, looking at her phone. Federico is sitting in a matching armchair flipping through a copy of *Essence* magazine that might be almost as old as Symone, while Lorenzo is watching the street outside.

Symone looks up when we rush into the room. "How'd it go?"

My knees are weak. "I think I just stood up to the Council."

Symone's eyes widen, and she shakes her head. "Girl, lemme call Zoe. She's gonna want to hear this."

<hr>

Salvatore

"We did it," Shae gasps, bending over to unzip her boots as soon as she walks into Zoe's apartment. "And they love you. They never liked my ex. Actually I don't think they like anyone the first time they meet them."

"I can be charming when I want to be." I laugh, reaching for her.

"Clearly." She dances away in her socks. I kick off my shoes and dart after her. "There was a moment when all I wanted to do was crawl onto your lap and kiss you."

"I don't know that your mother would have appreciated that, but I would have."

She lifts her left arm and unzips her dress. I pull off my jacket and drop it to the floor.

"They're going to want us to get married soon," she says.

"Is that what you want?"

She shimmies her dress over her shoulders and stops long enough to push it down her body. It catches on her hips, which seem wider than I remember, wider than just a few weeks ago. In fact, every part of her body looks fuller, thicker, and softer. I've been feeding her as much as I can, whatever she wants, making sure that she and our baby want for nothing. Just as I promised her aunts and mother I would.

"Eventually," Shae says, "but not any time soon. I don't need to get married just so no one wonders about when we conceived our baby."

My hand freezes. My belt is unbuckled, my pants unbuttoned. "Are you sure? If you're worried about how it looks—"

She laughs, reaching behind her back to unsnap her bra. "I don't care. The aunts might. My mom definitely does. But I don't. I'm not..." Her face falls along with her bra.

I rush to her and pull her against me. "Bella?"

She wraps her arms around my neck, her smile sad. "I realize that I'm not great at standing up for myself yet, but I...I want you to know that I can stand up for our baby. I don't care what anyone thinks about how fast our relationship is moving as long as we know our baby was created out of love."

"I've never doubted that."

"Really?" Her voice is delicately needy, a sound only she can make. Desire for her settles heavy in my balls.

I brush my mouth along hers. "Really, bella."

"How long do you want to stay here?"

I pull away. "Here?"

"Zoe's apartment, I mean. New York, too, I guess?"

"Do you...not want to stay here? I thought you wanted to be near your family."

"I did," she says. "I do. But I'm realizing that nearer than Italy doesn't have to be within walking distance." She smiles nervously as she says that.

"I understand." I begin to walk her back into the guest bedroom. Shae thought it would be strange to have sex in Zoe's bed. "We will find a place where we can be alone...but still close."

Shae smiles and kisses me quickly before backing out of my hold. "Driving distance close, but not need to spend the night driving distance." She tells me this while playing with the top of her underwear.

I would say yes to this no matter what. Besides, settling in New York is a cliché that someone like me cannot afford. But if Shae wants to slowly push her underwear over her hips and down her thighs to get me to agree...who am I to stop her?

Her panties finally drop to her feet at the bedroom door.

"Get on the bed." My voice is harder than I meant for it to sound, but my dick is aching, pulsing in my pants.

Shae turns and walks to the bed slowly, the beautiful flesh on her thighs and ass jiggling with every step. She sits demurely on the edge of the bed, but I shake my head.

"Get *on* the bed. On your back."

I unbutton my shirt and rip it from my body as Shae crawls to her knees and moves sensuously to the middle of the mattress.

Every peek of her brown lips and pink pussy makes me harder.

I move to the edge of the bed and slow down now, undress in unhurried, teasing movements of my own. Shae watches me, her hands moving over her front as her excitement grows. She cups her breasts when I take my undershirt off. Pinches her nipples when I push my trousers down my legs.

She bends her legs at the knees and then spreads them, watching me through her thighs as I stroke my cock through my underwear. When her delicate fingers begin to circle her clit, I shove my hand in my briefs and lightly stroke the length of my dick.

"Are you happy, bella?" I ask in a hoarse voice.

"Yes," she moans, her hips circling off the bed with that sound. "Are you happy?"

"Almost."

Her hand stops moving, and she frowns even though her eyes are still hazy with lust. "What?"

I push my underwear down my legs and then crawl

onto the bed. I kiss her shins and the top of each knee. I scrape my fingernails over her outer thighs. I kiss my way down her hand and then use my tongue to play with her clit.

"Oh God," she groans, lifting her hips again.

"Keep touching yourself," I whisper against her pussy and move my tongue over her lips.

She adds a second finger, circling that hard bud with a bit more pressure.

I use only the tip of my tongue to tease her lips. I kiss her opening, then shift my own hips into the mattress. The covers aren't warm and wet like her pussy, but I can wait. I miss the taste of her. The sound of her gentle sighs. The high-pitched moans. Her shaking thighs vibrating around my head while she comes. Pushing inside of her after that, when her pussy is dripping wet from my mouth and her orgasms, will be even sweeter.

Her fingers slide through my hair.

I need more.

I shove my hands under her ass and shove her pussy up against my face.

"Fuck," she cries out, moving her fingers against her clit faster now.

I use the flat of my tongue to take deep strokes, sliding between her lips, pressing into her opening, and licking down into the crack of her ass.

Her body jerks, and a small spray of her arousal splashes against my cheek.

I move my mouth back to her pussy, licking and sucking more of her from her opening.

She lets go of her clit and grabs the bedsheet.

I lick her like an ice cream and then fasten my entire mouth over her cunt.

She screams and shudders.

I focus on her clit, sucking her bud until the soft tremors are violently strong and her legs give way, and she collapses onto the bed. Now, I can use my fingers, working three into her from the start. She's wet enough. She's horny enough. I don't want to wait.

The next orgasm seems to go on forever. Until my mouth and chin are covered in her come, her thighs are wrapped around my face, her hands are holding my head against her pussy, and I'm fucking my hips into the mattress, close to coming along with her.

But I want to be inside her, and I back away. She whines in protest, but she's too weak to stop me.

I wipe my mouth with my hand and use it to stroke my dick. I won't last long, but I'll make her come on my shaft at least one more time. I can promise both of us that, at least.

I slip inside of her slow and steady. My back aches with the pressure, the need to slam into her again and again, as many times as we both can stand.

"Please," she groans, reaching for me. She grabs my shoulders and pulls me on top of her. She wraps her legs around my waist, desperate for the full weight of my body. She licks at my lips, tasting herself on my tongue as I crush my mouth against hers.

"Now I'm happy," I say, groaning as I start to move out of her then push inside again. "Now, I'm home."

Qadir

"Pops, you gotta stop ordering all this damn fig jam. It don't sell," I call from my perch on the floor.

"It *should* sell. It ain't my fault these white people coming in here don't have no damn taste."

I dropped by the import food shop my father owns to help him and my younger brother, Josh, stock the shelves with the new inventory. At my father's belligerent response, all I can do is sigh and roll my eyes in Josh's direction. We go through this every damn time. Josh shakes his head quickly, but not enough to draw dad's attention.

We live in the middle of a solidly lower middle-class Black neighborhood in Philadelphia, and a lot of our neighbors are hanging onto their homes and property values with all their might. My family is *not* lower middle-class, though. We're not even upper middle-class.

I mean, we put on like we are, and dad raised us not to flash our money, but I learned early that my financial life was nothing like my friends'. I've never once gone to bed hungry. I don't know the fear that can infect a home when someone loses their job and next month's mortgage payment is up in the air. I've never huddled near the kitchen when my mom was cooking dinner because the rest of the house was ice-cold. Actually, my mom is as much a fleeting memory in my life as my brothers' mothers as well, but that don't have much to do with class. We always had our dad, though. And it's hard to miss someone who never wanted to stick around anyway.

So, even though he makes stocking the shop a whole goddamn ordeal because he has a habit of ordering things for our Italian import shop that he *thinks* people should buy but not necessarily what our customers want, I still show up every week to help. Besides, we got to keep our cover strong.

If our family sometimes stands out in our neighborhood, our shop, Gastronomia Italiana, is even more of an anomaly. We only sell imported Italian foods that no one else in the state can access. Dad's connections and exclusive suppliers are so good that we deal with most of the Italian restaurants in Pennsylvania; the ones who want the best ingredients from Italy and don't care why a small import shop owned by a Black man is the only place to get what they need.

When people ask how my family came to own this shop — and many people have, including friends from school, customers, the local DEA agents pretending to be customers — me and my brothers learned early how to answer the question. Dad used to work at the shop when he was a teenager, and the owner had thought of him like a son. When he wanted to retire, he sold the shop to his favorite employee, and here we are.

It's close enough to the truth, which makes it a damn near indestructible lie.

Dad's tirade picks up out of nowhere, and I turn back to the shelves. "All these people want is that sugary ass tomato sauce and Nutella."

Dad is stocking a low shelf with dried fresh noodles that cost a fucking fortune to import and sell for more. That's where we should be putting our resources, but I don't have the energy to fight my dad on this for the three hundredth time.

I wish my older brother, Romeo, was here. Dad doesn't take any of our advice — which is why we got so many damn boxes of fig jam nobody wants in the stockroom — but Romeo has always been better at distracting dad from lecturing us, and I miss that right now. Without him, me and Josh just have to settle in for this lecture on the trash palate of Americans who like Olive Garden and jarred tomato sauce. I know this one practically by heart. Thankfully, dad takes his rant into the back storeroom, looking for another box to unpack.

The bell over the shop's front door rings out, and I stand from the bottom shelf, a jar of fig jam in each hand.

"Welcome to Gastronomia Italiana," Josh says brightly to the customer.

I cringe at his Italian pronunciation. He's the baby of

the family and dad's favorite. Has to be because dad would never let me or Romeo get away with anything less than perfect Italian.

I duck out of the aisle, smiling at the older white man. He has salt and pepper hair and thin wire-framed glasses. I don't recognize him, but I'm always on guard. He could be a regular customer, or he could be with the DEA. We'll see.

He's holding an adorable little girl in his arms, and I smile at her. She has the same light gray eyes as the older man, but her mama is definitely Black. That's as clear from her adorable round button nose as the butterfly barrettes anchoring the small pigtails at the top of her head. She locks eyes with me and smiles. I wave a jar of jam at her.

"Is your father here?" the man asks in a thick Italian accent.

That makes me nervous.

I see Josh climbing down from the ladder he was using at that question, but I don't let on. If anything, I smile wider. "Can we help you? We just got a new shipment of Tuscan fig jam."

The man smiles back. "I'll take it that means your father is here."

"We've got ten different kinds of pesto if you're looking for something special," Josh offers, inching closer.

"I'm looking for your father," the man says again, the little girl squirming excitedly in his arms.

"What the fuck are you doing here?" dad calls out, shocking the little girl so bad she bursts into tears.

Salvatore

"Do you feel good about yourself?"

"It was an accident. How was I supposed to know she would cry?"

"You raised three sons. How could you not know?"

"Can y'all fight later?" one of the younger men says as he inches closer with a lollipop in his hand.

"She can't have that much sugar," I say automatically. "My wife will kill me."

"Better you than us," he says, offering it to Mirabella tentatively. She reaches for it, and I bounce her in my arms, humming soothingly at her. The sweet stops her cries, but not the sweet little baby whimpers that I'll never get enough of. I pull a handkerchief from my pocket and wipe at her wet, chubby cheeks.

I hear the scoff, but I don't let it bother me. I'm too worried about wiping Bella's face and also praying that she won't want to unwrap that candy. She's just young enough to be charmed by the color and not recognize that it's edible. There's enough sugar in that thing to keep her up for three days.

Shae would actually kill me, and right while we're enjoying trying for another baby. I would love to avoid that.

Once Bella's face is dry, she clutches the candy to her chest and sinks into my arms, resting her head on my shoulder. I could cry, but I'll have to do that later.

I turn to see the man I came here to meet again.

He's standing across the shop from me, his two sons flanking each side. We're both so much older than the last time we saw one another, which feels like three lifetimes ago, but I think the same thing I thought then — that he looks exactly like a version of me. The Trovato genes are strong.

"È bello vederti, cugino," I say to Dante, the only family I have left.

"What'd he say?" one boy asks with bunched eyebrows.

"Cousin?" the other says, turning to his father. "Y'all are related?"

I smile as Dante rolls his eyes. I guess he can't pretend not to speak Italian to avoid me.

"Ah, shit," Dante hisses.

"Dai," I say, covering Bella's ear with my free hand. "Watch your mouth."

Katrina Jackson is a college professor by day and she writes erotica, erotic romance and historical fiction by weekend. She writes racially diverse and queer stories that show love and the world in all its beauty and diversity.

twitter.com/katrinajax

instagram.com/katjacksonbooks

amazon.com/author/katrinajackson

bookbub.com/authors/katrina-jackson

patreon.com/katrinajackson

Welcome to Sea Port

From Scratch

Inheritance

Small Town Secrets

Her Christmas Cookie

The Spies Who Loved Her

Pink Slip

Private Eye

Bang & Burn

New Year, New We

His Only Valentine

Bright Lights

Erotic Accommodations

Room for Three?

Neighborly

Love At Last

Every New Year

Heist Holidays

Grand Theft N.Y.E.

The Family

Beautiful and Dirty

The Hitman

The Enforcer

Dolci

The Don

Dolore

Bay Area Blues

Layover

Back in the Day

Patreon

Looking

My Darling, Theodore

Curriculum Vitae

Office Hours

Standalone stories

Encore

The Tenant

Sex Toy Soldier